What others are saying about *The Secret of Spirit Lake*

Patrick Gabridge strikes gold in this fast-paced summer adventure story. Tyra's summer at her eccentric grandfather's house takes an unexpected turn when she witnesses his obsession with old maps, bootlegging history, and buried treasure. As Tyra aids in her grandfather's treasure hunt—and embarks on her own journey to understand her adoptive family's history—she unearths a buried treasure that neither of them expected. *The Secret of Spirit Lake* has all the ingredients of a timeless classic, with a contemporary, relatable heroine readers will root for.

Diana Renn, author of *Tokyo Heist* and *Blue Voyage*

When Tyra is forced to leave her friends in the city for summer in the woods with a grandfather who's the master of mixed signals, she's pretty sure she'll die of boredom. She couldn't be more wrong—though dying is not out of the question in a town where the lure of long-lost treasure turns ordinary people ruthless. Gabridge weaves questions of family, identity, and belonging into a thrilling and increasingly propulsive tale that will have readers of all ages holding their breath till the last page.

David Valdes Greenwood, author of *Revengers*

The Secret of Spirit Lake

by
Patrick Gabridge

FIRST EDITION

ISBN: 978-0-9986982-2-9
Ebook ISBN: 978-0-9986982-3-6

Published by Pen and Pepper Press
Medford, MA
www.gabridge.com

For Kira

The Secret of Spirit Lake

Chapter One

KEEP OUT!

That was the first sign welcoming Tyra to Grandpa Rudy's house, as her dad turned their Subaru station wagon onto a narrow dirt path through the woods. The ruts in the driveway bounced them up off their seats and sent the beads at the ends of Tyra's braids clacking against each other so they sounded like a manic typewriter.

Every other tree hosted a sign: a black-and-orange GO BACK! and TRESPASSERS WILL BE PROSECUTED. Then: NO ENTRY—THIS MEANS YOU!

"*Sacrebleu*," muttered Tyra's mom. She spoke in French half the time now, as she and Tyra's dad prepared for their big trip to France. Their trip was the reason why Tyra was being forced to start her summer with a man who posted a sign that said ABANDON ALL HOPE, YE WHO ENTER HERE.

Usually Tyra's dad wore a grin inside his closely trimmed red beard. But now his lips were tightly pressed together, and wrinkles lined his forehead.

"It'll be all right, Dave," Tyra's mom said, as she pressed a hand against the ceiling to keep from smacking her head.

"I know."

"She can entertain herself just fine. Right?" Tyra's mom turned back to look at her, and Tyra couldn't hide her nervousness. "Don't worry, Grandpa Rudy will be happy to see you, honey."

"Are you sure?"

She'd only met him a few times. He hardly ever spoke and never smiled. He hadn't been to their house since they'd moved to the Roxbury neighborhood of Boston, and they'd never visited him either. Grandpa Rudy didn't like the big city.

Tyra's dad and Grandpa Rudy looked a lot alike, except for the scowling. Tyra always noticed when people in a family resembled each other. She was adopted and black, so she didn't look like anyone in her family. No one ever exclaimed, "Oh, you have your mother's hair and your father's nose!" Still, she had things from them on the inside, where it counted.

"I don't want to be marooned in the wilderness. Why can't I stay with Adriana or Déjà back home?"

"Adriana and Déjà's moms both work during the day. The day camp canceled on us, and there's no way we're letting the bunch of you girls run around the neighborhood all day, unsupervised."

"We're not babies. We're eleven years old."

"It's just for two weeks. You'll read books, swim in the lake, go out on Grandpa's boat. Get some fresh air and sunshine. It'll be fun. Then Grandma Feather will come get you, and you'll have the best summer ever," said her mom in her most soothing voice. Her dad nodded, as if he was convinced.

Tyra's mom was good at making things seem reasonable. She'd almost made sense when she'd explained to Tyra why they needed to spend the summer in France without her—Mom had a scholarship to do research on prosthetic limbs and Dad was teaching a class at some French film institute. And she'd almost made sense when she explained about Grandma Feather's schedule not lining up, and why they wouldn't let Tyra stay with her best friends. Almost.

Another sign appeared, this one without any writing, just a skull and crossbones.

#

They parked next to a weathered log cabin with a front porch that stretched across the house. Nearby sat a barn with peeling red paint, whose open doors revealed an oil-stained concrete floor, workbenches, a rusty pickup truck, and a yellow snowplow blade. A neat row of digging tools leaned against the side of the barn: shovels, spades, hoes, picks, and mattocks. Wheelbarrows and garden carts waited in the yard to be called to duty.

"He's still digging," Tyra's dad mumbled as they walked to the front steps.

"We all have our obsessions," Tyra's mom said reassuringly. Tyra's dad didn't look reassured.

In the gap between the house and the barn, bright light shimmered through trees—the sun shining off a lake.

"It's so lovely here," Tyra's mom said, putting her hand on Tyra's dad's arm. The way she wore her hair pulled back made her look young, more like a student than a professor, except for the streaks of gray in the chestnut brown. Tyra's parents looked out of place in the forest, all dressed up in their traveling clothes.

"You grew up here?" Tyra asked. She had trouble imagining her father, who loved the movie houses and coffee shops of the city, living in the middle of the woods.

"I have a hard time believing it myself. My dad built this place right before my mom died. I was almost your age." His gaze drifted over the cabin. "You'll be fine."

They climbed the steps onto the porch. The woods were eerily quiet.

"Stop," Tyra's dad said. They turned around and found themselves face-to-face with a tall, bearded old man dressed in dirty camouflage pants and a faded blue work shirt. In one hand, he held a broken-handled shovel. His eyes squinted ever so slightly, as if he were wondering who these people were or wishing they'd disappear. The two men stared at each other for a long time. No one breathed.

Finally, Tyra's mom had had enough. She walked up to Grandpa Rudy and gave him a big hug. He raised his eyebrows in surprise, and he almost smiled.

"Rudy, it's good to see you. Thank you so much for helping us out. You remember Tyra."

"Of course I do." Grandpa Rudy's voice sounded like he ate rocks for breakfast. He stuck out his hand to Tyra, and she shook it. His hand was rough and strong, and so big it swallowed hers right up. His expression reminded her of her dad when he was either serious or annoyed. Had Grandpa Rudy ever been happy?

#

The inside of the house was filled with shelves and carefully aligned stacks of books, file cabinets, and tools of all sorts. There wasn't a speck of dust or dirt anywhere. Tyra accidentally knocked over a book as she walked down the hall—*The Complete Public Enemy Almanac, 1920-1940*. In a flash, Grandpa Rudy picked it up and replaced it in its exact right spot. He raised an eyebrow at her, maybe wondering if she was always this clumsy.

He led them down the hall, past a small bathroom to a bedroom. "This will be your room. It was your dad's, a long time ago."

A narrow bed lay by the window. A neat line of books and a boom box with stacks and stacks of cassettes covered the top of a wooden desk. On the knotty pine walls hung posters of men with guitars and long hair and tight clothes. Some of them wore weird black-and-white makeup—big red letters in the corner of the poster said KISS. There was even a framed photo of a young version of her father, with long hair of his own and a guitar. Tyra had expected framed photos of Charlie Chaplin.

"KISS? *Très chic*," teased Tyra's mom, her bright gray eyes laughing.

"Don't scoff. They were very popular." Tyra's dad pulled her suitcase into the room and looked around. He turned to his father. "You haven't changed a thing."

"I don't need the space. Might as well leave it."

"Right. Well, Tyra, you have a little time capsule of the early '80s. The cassette player might still work. Maybe you'll find something you'd like to listen to."

"I don't think so." She noticed an enormous fish with sharp, pointy teeth mounted on the wall. "What is that?"

"Northern pike," Grandpa Rudy said. "Your dad was quite the fisherman when he was a boy." His voice carried a touch of pride.

"Those things are swimming in the lake? How am I supposed to sleep with that staring at me all night?" Tyra asked. Its glassy eyes bored through her.

"Don't worry," her mom said. "You'll get used to it."

Tyra didn't want to get used to having dead fish on the wall or weird pictures of '80s rock bands. She wanted to be back home with her friends. She crossed her arms and scowled.

Grandpa Rudy matched her with a scowl of his own. Tyra couldn't imagine that he liked kids. Not even a little. How was she going to survive two weeks here?

Finally, Tyra's dad started to fidget and said, "It took longer to get here than we expected, Dad, so we need to hurry back. Our flight leaves at seven."

Back at the car, Tyra's heart beat faster at the thought of staying with Grandpa Rudy. Were they really going to leave her here? Maybe it was all a big joke, to get her to behave and not be late for dinner.

"Thanks for watching her, Dad. You know how much I hate to impose on you, but every other plan fell through."

The men shook hands, and, as they faced each other, she could see that their noses matched almost perfectly.

"Humph," Grandpa Rudy said. "Feather will be here in two weeks, right?"

"Right. Don't worry," her dad said. Then he kissed Tyra on the cheek and ran his hands over her braids and pulled her up against his chest. "We love you, Tyra. We'll miss you more than you know."

Then Tyra's mom hugged her tight and whispered in her ear. "Don't worry, *ma chère*. He'll warm up to you. And soon Grandma Feather will spoil you rotten. You'll have the best summer ever."

Tyra tried not to feel the big lump in her throat as her mom and dad got in the car and disappeared down the driveway into the woods. She and Grandpa Rudy watched in silence as the dust settled back onto the driveway.

Chapter Two

In her new room, Tyra unpacked her suitcase and shoved her clothes into the empty dresser drawers. She unfolded a T-shirt in which she'd wrapped two small gifts that Déjà and Adriana had given her.

Yesterday, even as her mother had been calling for her to come in and finish packing, Tyra had laughed and skipped up the street behind her friends, a blur of brown arms and legs in the hot sunshine of the first real day of summer. Adriana liked to skip everywhere, which Tyra felt was immature, since they were about to enter sixth grade in the fall—skipping everywhere was something third graders would do. But on that day, it felt right.

They danced past faded brownstones and hulking three-family houses, past the older boys hanging in the square, warming in the sun like lanky lizards in baggy pants, and reached an empty lot fronted by orphaned stone steps left behind from a house that burned years ago. Nothing else remained of the house but a crumbling stone fireplace and the puddingstone foundation.

Tyra and her friends were not the only ones to hide things in the lot, now overgrown with tall weeds and decorated with the rusty skeleton of an old couch and tires that collected water and bred mosquitoes. Once they found a box of bullets. Tyra had considered telling her mother or father, but then they would have told her to stay out of the lot, and that would have ruined their fun.

Tyra loved the old buildings in her neighborhood. Mrs. Robichaud, her fifth-grade teacher at St. Matthews, took them on a field trip through Roxbury and told them story after story about the places they walked past every day. Just down the street, a huge brick building had the words *Fellowes Athenaeum* carved into its granite top. Almost a hundred and fifty years ago, it was one of the first public libraries in the country. Now it was a Baptist church. Ever since their field trip, Tyra saw her neighborhood differently, curious about the stories that lurked in the attics and foundations on every block. Stories made everything fresh and alive.

Adriana pushed through the weeds to the fireplace, looking around to make sure no one was watching. With a jingle of her ever-present charm bracelet, she waved Tyra and Déjà over. Adriana wriggled a loose stone out of the chimney—one of their special hiding places—and pulled out an ancient metal cracker box, whose writing and picture had long since faded.

"We got you something," Déjà said.

Tyra opened the container eagerly. Inside, she found a red Swiss Army knife and a blue plastic whistle.

"If you're gonna be in the woods, we thought you should have these," said Adriana.

"Yeah, so, like, if you get lost or anything, you can blow the whistle. I saw that on a nature show," said Déjà. "And everyone needs a knife in the wilderness."

"It was my brother's," Adriana said, "from when he was a little kid." They all got quiet, which is what people did whenever anyone mentioned Adriana's brother, because he was dead, and it was important to be respectful of the dead, even if they died a while ago.

"Thanks," Tyra said, and she hugged her friends as tightly as she could. "But I'm not going to get lost in the woods."

"I hope not," said Déjà. "They got bears and all kinds of stuff up there."

"They don't, do they?" asked Adriana. Her family was from Puerto Rico, and Tyra was pretty sure they didn't have bears there. There certainly weren't any bears in Roxbury, not even in the Franklin Park Zoo.

"You'd better text us every day." Tyra's parents had finally agreed to let her have a cell phone, but she was nowhere near as fast at texting as Déjà.

"We'll be thinking about you when we're at the pool, and you have to swim in a lake, with the fish and the weeds. Poor Tyra," said Adriana.

Now Adriana and Déjà were miles and miles away. How could Tyra bear a whole summer away from them? Tyra and Déjà looked so much alike that sometimes people thought they were sisters, so they worked on making their laughs and smiles and hands move in the same way, to feel even more like they could be. What would happen if she missed the whole summer with them? Her friends would never forget her, but Tyra worried that by the end of the season, they might all be different.

She looked out the window at the barn and the thick, dark forest and slipped the whistle and knife into her pocket.

#

She wandered out to the screened-in back porch and saw the lake and a wooden dock just a short walk down a sandy path lined with a few small trees and bushes. Tiny waves whispered at the shore. Grandpa Rudy sat at a table, studying several maps, one of which was yellowed with age. When he heard Tyra slide open the screen door, he flipped over the maps to hide them from her.

"Hi," she said meekly. Tyra loved maps. What did they show? But first things first. "How do I get onto your Wi-Fi? Mom and Dad got me a cell phone, and I want to text my friends, but there's no signal here."

"Yeah, cell phones don't work up here too well."

"How do I connect to the Wi-Fi?"

"I don't have anything like that."

No Wi-Fi! It'd be like she disappeared from the face of the earth. At least she had some games and music downloaded, to help her stay sane. But what about her friends?

"Can I use your computer to email my friends? They expect to hear from me every day."

Grandpa Rudy pulled at his beard, which must have once been the same color as her dad's but was now completely gray.

"I don't have a computer."

"What?"

"No computer, no TV. None of that junk. Never saw the need for it."

"How do you live?"

"I get by."

Two weeks with no Internet, no television, nothing? Her friends would think she'd been eaten by bears.

Her mom and dad had never mentioned anything about this. Now they'd dumped her off to go have fun, while she was stuck here with nothing to do, cut off from the world. What was the French word for *unfair*?

Tyra's mom and dad had been a lot happier with each other ever since they started making plans and brushing up on their French. Many of Tyra's friends had divorced parents, and before the trip, she worried that her parents weren't happy enough to stay together. They got so busy with work that they didn't see each other much, and sometimes they didn't seem to like each other. But the trip had made everything different. So as much as she resented it, she knew it was important that they go.

In two weeks, Grandma Feather would rescue her. Grandma Feather was awesome. Even now she was off rock climbing and surfing. Dad called her an old hippie. She dressed in funky clothes and didn't like to wear shoes and had a huge garden, with a million bird feeders. She'd promised Tyra they would paint watercolors every morning and drink herbal tea and bask in the sun. Grandma Feather visited at least twice a year, no matter what, and always remembered Tyra's birthday and her adoption day, and would call to find out about the robot she'd built for her science project or to shore up her courage before a chorus concert. When Tyra visited her, Grandma Feather always made brownies and shredded chicken burritos, because they were Tyra's favorites.

Tyra craned her neck for a peek at Grandpa Rudy's maps. "What are your maps of?"

"Nothing that would interest you. Old stuff."

"I love old maps. My teacher Mrs. Robichaud showed us maps of Roxbury before it became part of Boston. The Bartlett pear was named after a man who had an orchard on Bartlett Street, right near my house. I started a map collection. I already have one of Roxbury, back when it was its own town. I have three maps on the wall of my room: Roxbury, Massachusetts, and one of the United States."

"These maps are none of your business." He rolled them up, took them inside the house, and locked them in one of the cabinets. Tyra followed right on his heels. "Let me guess," he said, with a little less fire now, "you want dinner."

"Yes, please." Maybe saying please and thank you would soften up Grandpa Rudy. Though that seemed impossible. What was so important about those maps?

"I remember how kids are. When your dad was growing up, he was like a tiger with a tapeworm." Grandpa Rudy walked into the kitchen, where he began poking through a cupboard. "Had to fix the motor on the boat this morning, so I didn't get to the store." He took down two cans, dumped something gross and smelly into a pot, and lit the stove with a match. Tyra's mom, even though she was busy teaching engineering students about artificial knee joints, never cooked out of cans.

"What is that?"

"Chili. What did you think?"

"It smells like dog food." The words came out before Tyra could stop herself.

He leaned down to smell it and wrinkled his nose. "You could be right. Wouldn't surprise me if Paul over at the store tried to pull something sneaky. But it says chili on the label, so let's assume it's chili. Guess you're used to gourmet down in Boston. We'll go to town tomorrow and find something that suits your palate."

"Shouldn't we have some vegetables?" Tyra believed in balanced meals, and she didn't think she'd be able to eat much of the chili anyway.

"Why not? We'll make a feast of it." He took down a can of corn and dumped it into the chili. Tyra tried not to grimace.

Grandpa Rudy showed Tyra the bowls and silverware so she could set the table. Through the big picture window in the dining room, they could see the lake beginning to glow pink from the sunset.

As Tyra picked at her food, Grandpa Rudy watched her closely, as if she was some sort of alien from another planet. She smiled and pretended to like the chili and corn.

"You a sound sleeper?" he asked suddenly.

"I guess so."

"Sometimes city folk get all worked up by noises in the woods at night. It's not as quiet out here as folks think. If you hear something, it's nothing, just raccoons and possums banging around. Nothing to fret about. Just turn over and go back to sleep. Don't get out of bed. Understand?"

Tyra nodded and swallowed a big drink of water to wash down the chili. How loud were those noises were going to be?

Chapter Three

That night, Tyra heard banging out by the barn. *Clank, bang, CLANK.* She buried her head under the covers. Grandpa Rudy had been serious—it *was* loud and annoying. Stupid raccoons. Could this summer get any worse? She couldn't sleep like this.

Then she wondered, could it be a bear? She would love to tell her friends she'd seen an actual bear.

More banging. Her curiosity took hold of her, and she sat up and looked out the window.

It wasn't a bear. It was something much stranger. There, under the dim yellow light from the barn, was Grandpa Rudy. He wore work clothes and had a bright light strapped to his hat. He tossed a shovel into a garden cart brimming with tools. He grabbed the handles and pushed the cart across the yard and onto a narrow path leading into the forest. In an instant, he vanished into the darkness.

What was he doing out there? Did it have anything to do with those secret maps? She tried waiting for him to come back, but her eyes wouldn't stay open.

#

The next morning, after breakfast, Grandpa Rudy declared that they would take the boat into town for groceries. The town lay directly across and down the lake, almost a mile away, but by car, it was more than a half-hour drive.

Tyra followed Grandpa Rudy down the sandy path to the dock. Spirit Lake stretched out in front of them, fresh and bright in the morning sun, the tiny waves breaking the light into a billion sparkles. Tyra took a deep breath, and the air tasted crisp and clean. She understood why someone might want to spend part of a summer in this place. If Déjà and Adriana had been there, she might have allowed herself to smile a little.

Grandpa Rudy tossed some square seat cushions into the aluminum fishing boat tied to the dock. It was sturdy and plain, with bare metal benches in the bow, center, and stern, and a pair of weathered wooden oars in the middle. An outboard motor was bolted to the back, the white plastic casing weathered yellow from years in the sun.

"Get on board," Grandpa Rudy instructed, as he untied the ropes that held the front and back of the boat to the dock.

Tyra stepped down into the boat a little gingerly, and it rocked. She'd spent some time in kayaks on the Charles River with her father back home. They were a lot tippier, but also a lot closer to the water. She sat down on one of the seat cushions in the middle of the boat, where it felt steadiest. Grandpa Rudy stepped aboard and sat on the stern bench.

"Ever drive one of these?" he asked.

"Me? No."

"Might as well learn while you're here. Come on back." He shifted over and she joined him, the boat's rocking making her nervous with every step.

"Don't worry, you're not going to tip us over," he said. "Now pay attention." He showed her the metal gas can, the lever to change the motor from forward to reverse, and the choke. It was a lot to remember.

"Once you've got everything set up, you give this starter cord a good yank. Come on, grab it." He guided her hand to a black plastic handle on the motor. "Go ahead. Pull."

She pulled the handle and the attached cord slowly out of the engine. Nothing happened.

"Put some muscle into it this time. Like you really mean it. Show it who's boss."

She gave the starter cord a hard yank, and this time the engine roared to life. She'd done it!

Grandpa Rudy flipped a lever and they inched forward. Then he did something crazy—he stepped forward and sat on the center bench, leaving her alone by the motor.

"What are you doing?" she asked.

"You're going to drive us there."

"Me? But I don't know how."

"Just take us straight ahead. We're heading to that town way over there. Steer using the tiller stick."

She tried to steer but nudged the nose of the boat back the wrong way.

"Outboards are strange—you have to steer right to go left. Right to go left. No. The other way."

Tyra swerved the boat in the other direction and got the boat pointed towards town. Grandpa Rudy leaned forward to point at the stick in her hand. "Okay. Let's pick up the pace. Rotate that to give it a little gas."

She twisted the throttle and shot the boat forward, raising the nose up into the air, tossing Grandpa Rudy off his feet. "Not that much!"

He dusted off the cobwebs and dirt as he pulled himself back onto the bench. He did not look pleased. Tyra hid her smile.

The boat surged forward over the water, with a tiny bump-bump-bump over the light chop. The wind pressed against Tyra's face and filled her ears, and her smile worked its way outside for the first time since she'd arrived in Spirit Lake. Even Grandpa Rudy relaxed and tilted his head back to soak up the sun, like a lion. Tyra could see her father in the shape of his eyes. Maybe her father and mother were on a boat in Paris or eating dinner in a café. She hoped they would call soon. Missing them made the sunny day feel cloudy.

The small town across the lake grew closer. It wasn't much of a town, mostly a cluster of houses along the shore, each with a dock, and there was a lodge with a beach and a long row of tiny lakefront cabins. A marina and a general store separated the town from the lodge. The marina's faded sign said IKE's in big red letters.

Grandpa Rudy motioned for Tyra to slow down. "I'll take it from here. You can practice bringing us into the dock at my place." They switched seats, and the boat tipped back and forth and swerved when Tyra released her hand from the tiller. Tyra gripped the gunwales tightly, certain they were going to capsize, her stomach doing flip-flops. But Grandpa Rudy calmly steered them to the marina.

Another fishing boat was already tied up at the marina's main dock, so Grandpa Rudy pulled up on the opposite side. A burly, red-faced man watched a wiry boy about Tyra's age pumping gas for the boat. The man's hat and vest bristled with so many fishing flies and lures he looked like a strange animal with a coat of colorful feathers and hooks. His wide-bottomed boat had shiny black sides and unblemished gray vinyl decking with two swivel chairs.

"Tie us up to that cleat," Grandpa Rudy barked at Tyra as they bumped against the dock. She wasn't sure exactly what a cleat was, but figured it had to be one of the metal brackets sticking off the dock. She jumped onto the dock and wound the bow line around the cleat. Grandpa Rudy frowned and waved Tyra down to his end of the boat, where he showed her how to wrap the rope around the cleat in an overlapping figure eight. "It'll stay tight that way, and it's easy to undo," Grandpa Rudy said, shaking his head. "Don't they teach kids anything in the city?"

Well, not about boats, thought Tyra as she retied the rope.

"Hi, Rudy. Nice to see you," the red-faced man said, offering his hand.

"Hiya, Ted. Just up from the city?"

"Yeah. Finally up for the season. I'm about to head out and drown a few worms. And try a new lure or two." Ted proudly pointed to some plastic fish with sharp hooks attached to his hat. His every move generated a high-pitched jingle, as the hooks tapped against each other. "I've got a new bird book, too, so even if the fish aren't biting, I'll still see something interesting." He patted a big pair of binoculars slung around his neck.

Tyra thought that, with all that gear strapped on, he'd better hope he didn't fall overboard. She waited for Grandpa Rudy to introduce her, but he didn't even look at her.

"Maybe this year you'll catch the big one you're always after," Grandpa Rudy said.

"And maybe Rudy will finally come to his senses." This came from a gray-haired woman striding up the dock with a picnic basket. She wore jeans and a polo shirt with SPIRIT LAKE LODGE written across the front. Grandpa Rudy took a quick breath and stood a little straighter.

"I don't know what you're talking about, Lily."

The woman laughed. "Well, let's hope you figure it out, before it's too late." She handed the basket to Ted. "Here's lunch and some bait, but you know they won't be biting in the heat of the day." Then she noticed Tyra. "Rudy Palmer, I believe you've brought a visitor." She looked straight at Tyra, and Tyra could tell this was the kind of woman who makes friends quickly and knows how everyone is connected to everyone else. In Tyra's neighborhood, Mrs. Starling was like that—she ran the community garden and organized neighborhood cleanups, and once she brought in a truck that sold used Rollerblades to kids for two dollars a pair.

"It'll take him forever to remember his manners and introduce us, so I'll just go ahead. I'm Lily, and that's Cory, my grandson. He helps me in the summertime. We run the Spirit Lake Lodge. This is Ted McCoy, one of our regular lodge guests. You must be Tyra."

"How did you know?"

"Your father called me. Wanted me to keep an eye on you while you're staying with your grandfather. Let me know if you need anything."

It made Tyra feel warm inside to know that her dad had taken the trouble to make sure someone else was watching over her.

"Dave called you?" Rudy said suspiciously. "He didn't say anything to me. No need to stick your nose in. I've got the situation under control."

"Oh, I'm sure you do," Lily said.

"You know my dad?" Tyra asked. He'd never mentioned anything about Lily or Spirit Lake Lodge, but he didn't talk much about his childhood.

"Oh, good lord, how many hours did he spend at our lodge? Never missed a movie night, I promise you that. And I haven't seen many children who insist on fishing and reading a book at the same time. But now he's all grown. France for the summer, isn't that a dream come true? You and Cory look like you're about the same age. Are you eleven?"

"That's right."

"I knew it. Rudy, you need to bring her by, once she's settled. Cory will be glad to have another youngster around."

Cory, in the meantime, had finished gassing up Ted's boat and now stood near Tyra, first balanced on one foot, then the other. He and Tyra were almost the same height. He was deeply tanned by the sun, almost as dark as Adriana, though with his freckles and bushy white-blond hair, he definitely didn't look

Puerto Rican. He popped down into a handstand, walked a few feet on his hands, then snapped back to his feet with a smile.

"Do you like to fish?" Cory asked. He had the same straightforward gaze as his grandmother, and he looked at Tyra with hopeful curiosity.

"I've never gone before," Tyra confessed.

"It'll be an adventure. It's important to have at least one adventure every day, or else you'll slowly die of boredom and not even know it."

"I guess so."

Cory jumped straight up into the air and spun himself around. "I can do a three-sixty no problem, but I'm shooting for a five-forty," he said. Tyra had never met anyone quite like Cory. If her friends had been there, they would have given him a wide berth.

"I know where all the good spots are. This year, I'm going to catch all fifteen kinds of fish that live in Spirit Lake. I'm already up to seven."

"Some say he's the best guide on the lake," said Ted, as he climbed down into his boat, jingling with each step. Cory hopped on one foot across the dock and handed Ted the picnic basket and his fishing gear.

Grandpa Rudy watched all this activity, looking a little uncomfortable. "She's not going to be here long. Just two weeks."

"Let's make the most of it, then," Lily said. "Why don't you come to the lodge for dinner? That way the poor girl can eat at least one decent meal while she's here."

"Well . . . I . . ."

"Rudy." Her voice was a little softer this time, which made Grandpa Rudy act even more nervous.

"We'll see. Come on, Tyra. We need to buy some groceries." Grandpa Rudy looked down at Lily, since she was a foot shorter than he was, but he could only meet her eyes for an instant before he stumbled away. Tyra could swear he was blushing behind his beard.

"When I finish my chores tomorrow, I'll come by and maybe we can go fishing," Cory suggested.

Tyra wasn't sure how she felt about worms and fish, but she didn't want to stay in Grandpa's cabin all day, so she said that would be a great idea. She wanted to ask Cory if he had Internet, so she could email Adriana and Déjà, but Grandpa Rudy was waiting impatiently at the end of the dock.

"Come on, we haven't got all day," he said.

Lily put a reassuring hand on Tyra's shoulder as she passed by. "Don't worry. He isn't as grizzly as he seems." And then, quietly, "Just don't get between him and his shovels, okay?"

#

Tyra entered the store right behind her grandfather. It resembled the corner store from back home, with groceries, snacks, aspirin, and soda, but all of that was blended with the contents of a hardware store and a bait shop. Not far from the door, across from the checkout counter, four old men drank coffee and ate doughnuts around a small table. They were loud and laughing, and one of them called out to Grandpa Rudy, "Hey, look, it's the ghost of Rudy Palmer." He barely acknowledged them.

When Grandpa Rudy reached down to pick up a plastic basket for the groceries, the men saw Tyra and instantly fell silent. They stared at her with unfriendly eyes. She cautiously took cover behind her grandfather, who kept gathering items for their dinner. She could feel the eyes of the old men on her as she walked down the aisle. She tried to distract herself by noticing the lawn chairs and fish-scaling knives and toilet paper, but the silence grated on her. No one said a word.

Once he'd filled the basket, Grandpa Rudy walked them to the checkout counter, where the clerk rang up their purchases. His fingers on the cash register keys was the only sound in the store. Grandpa Rudy kept his back to the men, staring at the clerk instead, a balding man with a few strands of hair combed over the top of his head. The clerk kept his eyes fixed on the groceries and his cash register.

Grandpa Rudy leaned close to the clerk and whispered, "Did that metal detector come in?"

The man looked at Grandpa Rudy, then at Tyra, paused, and finally answered, "Not yet."

"That last one was a piece of junk."

The clerk nodded but said nothing.

Grandpa Rudy paid, and as he and Tyra carried their bags toward the door, one of the men at the table finally spoke. His face was leathery and wrinkled from the sun, and he held his coffee cup with thick, stubby fingers.

"So, this is that black girl Dave adopted."

Grandpa Rudy stopped and turned to face the men. He shifted his feet nervously. "Yeah. Just up here for a bit."

Tyra waited for Grandpa Rudy to introduce her or say something more, but instead he just looked at the men, one at a time, and walked out the door. "Come on, let's go," he said to her.

As Tyra hurried out behind him, the men began speaking all at once, an energetic mix of "Whoever would've thought," "She's black all right," "Damn shame," "World's a funny place," and "Never seen one up here."

Tyra scrunched her face and clamped herself shut inside. Did Grandpa Rudy hear what they were saying? Were these his friends? The words pushed hard against the closed door, as if they wanted to follow Tyra down the dock.

And then one last phrase drifted out: "Wonder if she knows about the treasure?"

Treasure? What treasure?

They loaded into the boat, and Grandpa Rudy drove them home. Tyra sat on the front seat, as far from him as she could get. As curious as she might be about some sort of treasure, she was even angrier at him and his friends.

There were plenty of white people in Boston, and she and her parents had traveled to Washington, D.C., Chicago, New York City, Florida, and Cape Cod. Sometimes people gave her family a second look, but rarely did someone stare. At home, she was one of lots of brown and black faces in the neighborhood and at school. Her white parents were the ones who stood out in Roxbury. When she started kindergarten, kids would ask why her parents were white, and Tyra always explained, "They were just born that way." She wasn't the only one with a white parent, anyhow.

The way those men stared at her made Tyra want to be anywhere else on earth. All she'd needed was for Grandpa Rudy to help, at least a little. But he didn't.

Grandpa Rudy's eyes stayed focused straight ahead, staring out at the lake. She wanted to say, "Why didn't you stick up for me? Why didn't you claim me?" But she couldn't bring herself to speak, not when he was sitting there, like he was made of stone.

Even the noise of the wind and the motor couldn't fill the silence between them.

Chapter Four

At dinner time, Grandpa Rudy put a plate in front of Tyra bearing a hamburger, pickle, fries, fresh green beans, and even a salad. "Real food," he said, as he took his seat. "Nothing out of a can."

Tyra still couldn't bring herself to look at him. He should have said something at the store, something to prove he was on her side and that he wasn't embarrassed by who she was. Did he not understand, even a little?

"I'm not hungry," she mumbled.

"Tyra. I know I'm. . . Sometimes I don't say the right things. And I—"

"I *said* I'm not hungry."

"Suit yourself," he said, taking a big juicy bite out of his burger. "But those french fries won't be as good when they're cold."

The burger smelled like summer, and the bun had sesame seeds on it, exactly the way she liked it. The slice of dill pickle was the kind her dad would buy. Tyra's stomach pinched with hunger. But there was a kernel of something deep inside, an ache, that wouldn't feel any better by eating burgers and fries.

The phone rang, really rang, as if it had a bell inside, and Tyra saw that it was the kind with a dial that spins around. Maybe it was her parents calling from France, and she could tell them that she needed to go to Pennsylvania to Grandma Feather's *right now*. Two days at Spirit Lake was more than enough.

Grandpa Rudy answered the phone. "Hello? Oh, hello, Amanda. You made it there all right? Good. Oh, we're doing fine. Where's Dave? The two of you are jumping in with both feet, aren't you? Of course. Right. Oh. Oh my goodness. That's a long way. Is she all right? Well, that's a relief. What hospital? But how will she . . . ? Oh." A long silence. "Of course. It'll be fine. Sure. Yep. We'll manage. Don't you worry."

He looked troubled as he handed the phone to Tyra, who waited anxiously by his side.

"Hello?" Tyra breathed.

"Hi Sweetie, it's Mom." She sounded tired and far away. "How are you doing at your grandfather's house?"

"I'm okay." Tyra was old enough to know that something bad had happened. An accident in Paris? "Did something happen to Dad?"

"No, we're fine. Paris is beautiful. Your dad will be back any second—his class started today. I start work tomorrow.

"Honey, I just talked to Auntie Beth. Grandma Feather has had an accident. She's fine, so don't worry. She had a fall while rock climbing in Mexico and smashed her elbow. She's going to need surgery and some time to recover."

"I'm sure I can help take care of her," Tyra said. She tried to think of any books she'd read that might have tips on how to nurse her grandmother back to health, but mostly she read stories about detectives and kids who could cast magic spells.

"Well, it's going to be pretty involved. She's going to stay with Auntie Beth while she recuperates. She'll be there for the rest of the summer." Auntie Beth was Tyra's mother's sister. She lived in Florida, in a condo near the beach. They liked to visit her in March, when Boston was cold and gloomy.

"How am I going to get down there?"

"Auntie Beth doesn't have much room, and she'll have her hands full with your grandmother." Tyra's mom took a deep breath. "Grandpa Rudy said you can stay with him for the rest of the summer."

Grandpa Rudy sat down at the table and stared at his plate.

"I can sleep on the floor at Auntie Beth's, in a sleeping bag. I won't be any trouble. I can help take care of Grandma. I can't stay here all summer. You don't understand. But I can't. Please. Please. *Please?*"

"We might not stay away for the whole summer. I need to complete my research, but your dad might come back early. He has to finish teaching his class, though, and that's four weeks. You'll be fine."

Tyra cupped her hand around the receiver and whispered, "Come get me and bring me home. I don't like it here."

"I'm sorry it's not what you wanted. Grandma Feather will miss seeing you so much. Dad and I will find a way to get you earlier. But you have to be patient."

"But—"

"This is the way it has to be, Tyra."

"Okay." Tyra knew her mom and dad were supposed to take small trips around Europe together, which had been a perfect plan, before now. She wanted them to be happy, but she didn't want to stay here one more day.

"We'll call again soon. I love you, Tyra. You'll be fine."

And that was it. The summer had turned into a total, complete, enormous disaster. Tyra hung up the phone and joined Grandpa Rudy in staring at dinner without eating it.

"It's not fair," Tyra said.

"No, it's not."

Tyra's hands curled into fists. "I didn't come here to ruin your life or embarrass you. You don't want me here. No one does. Don't worry, you'll never have to take me into that store again."

She ran to her room, slammed the door, and flopped onto the bed. She tried so hard not to cry—she beat her fists on the pillow; she scrunched up her face; she pinched the skin on her arms. But when faced with the worst possible summer with the worst possible grandfather in the worst possible place in the world, sometimes weeping is the only answer.

#

Tyra sat on the end of the dock playing a game on her phone. In the quiet edge of night, the lake stretched out in front of her like a mirror, reflecting a violet sky. A single bright star shone over the mountains, waiting for others to follow. Tyra reached into a bowl of pretzels and grabbed a handful. Grandpa Rudy was inside on the back porch, studying his secret maps, lost in his own private little world.

The crunch of the pretzels and the sound of the game rattled the twilight calm, but she didn't care. She didn't care about the beauty of the lake or the mountains or the trees. She just wanted to be home with her friends, listening to the pounding bass from cars rolling by, or smelling her mother's cooking, or hearing her dad washing the dishes and reminding her to finish clearing the table.

She reached down for another handful of pretzels and brushed a furry hand. She heard a quick chirp and turned to see a huge raccoon sitting next to her, helping himself to her snack.

Tyra shrieked and jumped to her feet, backing away from the creature. The raccoon popped straight into the air, puffed up like a huge hairy blowfish. It gave a shriek of its own, and Tyra backed up one step too far. She teetered on the edge of the dock, then fell into the lake.

The water was cold and black and over her head. Gasping and sputtering, she reached up and grabbed the edge of the dock. In the dim light, the raccoon skittered off into the woods. With all her strength, Tyra pulled herself out of the ice-cold water.

Her phone was gone, lost at the bottom of the lake. Tyra's growl-moan-scream echoed across the water.

Chapter Five

Hours later, Tyra lay in bed in the dark, holding her breath. Waiting.

She slipped from under the covers and tugged on her sneakers. Would he go into the woods again tonight? She peered cautiously out the window. The sodium light over the barn buzzed and flickered, casting a sickly glow over the peeling paint.

A scratch of boots on gravel. A clank of metal on metal.

Grandpa Rudy pushed the battered garden cart filled with picks and shovels across the yard, just like he had last night. Did he do this every night? With his beard and scowl, he was like a troll or a strange woodsman out of a fairy tale.

Tonight, she didn't hesitate. If her parents were going to dump her in Spirit Lake and ruin her entire summer, she needed to know what was going on. Tyra ran down the hall in her nightgown and sneakers, slid open the door to the back porch, and pranced on tiptoes across the weeds and gravel.

Grandpa Rudy was already in the woods, pushing his cart down the thin path by the light of his headlamp, over rocks and roots. He moved with a fierce intensity, a dark shadow in the even darker woods.

Tyra scurried after him as quietly as she could, trying not to breathe too loudly. What sorts of things lurked in the woods at night? It never got this dark in Roxbury, and if any place did, people knew they shouldn't go there.

Was Grandpa Rudy digging something up, or was he burying something? What was it?

She caught her sneaker on a root and tripped, sending her straight to the ground. All the air whooshed out of her. She froze. Up ahead, Grandpa Rudy heard the sound and whirled around, a shovel raised up high. His lamp shone back toward her like a spotlight, sweeping back and forth, but Tyra pressed herself to the ground.

"Who's there?" her grandfather growled through his bushy beard.

The sound of her heartbeat pounded so loud in her ears, she thought he'd surely hear it. He took a step in her direction and stopped, his head cocked, listening.

The light passed back and forth against the trees and bushes, just over her head. She tried to ignore how much her knee hurt from banging it on a rock when she fell. Her eyes watered. She bit her lip.

Finally, he turned back to his cart and hurried away, his light growing dim as he moved farther into the woods.

She slowly stood, feeling more alone than she had at any time in the past few lonely days. Grandpa Rudy's light flickered dimly off the trees like the mist of a ghost, growing fainter by the second. Tyra couldn't even see her feet on the path anymore. Behind her, she could barely make out the lamp by the barn, like a solitary star in a black sky. If she went any farther and didn't catch up with Grandpa Rudy, she'd be lost in the dark forest. With the bears and the raccoons and the coyotes. Maybe her ruined summer *could* get even worse.

She looked ahead to find her grandfather, but he'd vanished.

Tyra crept back to the cabin, feeling her way down the path with her feet, snagging her nightgown on branches and bushes. At last, she worked her way into the clearing by the barn.

Next time she'd be prepared.

Chapter Six

In the morning, Tyra washed the cut on her knee from when she'd tripped last night. She found a Band-Aid in the bathroom and hoped Grandpa Rudy wouldn't ask how she hurt herself. He probably wouldn't notice anyway.

Tyra made herself cereal in the kitchen while her grandfather snored on the couch, as loud as a chainsaw. She'd never heard anyone snore so loudly. He clearly hadn't changed clothes after he got home—bits of sand and pine needles spotted the knees of his olive-green work pants. A dark-red cut ran across the top of his knuckles. What was he up to?

Tyra finished her breakfast and wondered what he'd do if she poured the milk from her cereal bowl onto his head. That would be one way to stop the snoring.

Instead, she decided to go outside and explore. Just as she was about to open the screen door, there was Cory, his hand poised for a knock.

"Psst," Tyra whispered. "Don't." She gestured toward her snoring grandfather, who looked like he'd never move from the couch in a thousand years.

Together they walked away from the house and the racket, to the dock, where a battered blue fishing boat labeled SPIRIT LAKE LODGE in bold black letters was tied next to Rudy's.

"Does he always snore like that?" Cory asked.

"I don't know. If he keeps doing it, I might need earplugs. Especially now that I'm stuck here for the rest of the summer."

"What happened?"

"My grandmother got hurt, so I have to stay here. I'm trying to convince my parents to come home early, but they can't get away."

"There are worse places to be stuck." Cory jumped up onto one of the dock's pilings and tried to balance, flapping his arms to keep from falling.

"Easy for you to say. Your grandmother is so nice. You're not cooped up with a crazy old man." She checked to make sure that Grandpa Rudy wasn't watching, though the sound of his snoring made it obvious. "He sneaks out late at night, with all kinds of tools. Shovels and picks. He's digging for something."

"Maybe he's burying bodies. Or hunting for buried treasure."

Tyra lowered her voice to a whisper. "I started to follow him last night."

"No way. What did you see?"

"Nothing. I lost him in the dark. He heard me, but he didn't see me."

"What if he'd caught you?"

"I don't even want to think about it." Then Tyra had an idea. "Let's look at his tools. Maybe they'll give us a clue."

Together they ran to the barn and found the shovel and pick Grandpa Rudy had used last night. Tyra touched the dirt caked on the blade—it was still moist. "I wish I had a magnifying glass, like Sherlock Holmes," she said. "He would notice something about this. It's sort of sandy. Maybe it's from down by the shore."

Tyra examined the top of the workbench. Grandpa Rudy must have been too tired to put everything away when he got home. On the bench were battery-powered lamps and a long black tube.

"What's this?" She opened the end of the tube and pulled out a set of rolled maps.

Cory peered over her shoulder. "Maybe they're treasure maps."

"I learned how to read maps in school," Tyra said. She searched for the legend. "This one is of Spirit Lake and was made in nineteen twenty-eight. The year of any map is important, because landscapes change over time. That's what my teacher told us."

Cory pointed to a box drawn in pencil on the edge of Spirit Lake. "That's your grandfather's cabin, right here."

"What are these?" Tyra asked, running her finger over various Xs and boxes drawn on the map, mostly along the shore, but also in the woods.

"I don't know. But we could find out." Cory's eyes gleamed.

"Now?"

"I've got my boat. I was coming to see if you wanted to go fishing."

"I don't know. If he sees the map missing . . ."

"We'll study it and leave the map here. See this X? This is in the next cove over, past Loon Point. We'll go look around and catch a few fish to cover our tracks. First, we'll put these back where we found them."

Tyra and Cory studied the map and then she slid it back with the others into the tube and placed it on the workbench.

"No," Cory said. "The tube was on the other side of the lamps."

"Are you sure?"

"Definitely."

Tyra moved the map. "Let's go," she said, taking one last glance at the barn, to make sure everything was exactly as they'd found it.

#

As they sped away, Cory pointed at a boat anchored in an arm of the lake close to Grandpa Rudy's cabin. "There's Ted," Cory yelled over the roar of the engine. "That's his favorite fishing spot. I keep telling him there's not much around there, but he's convinced he's going to catch a big one. He's out there all the time. That island over there is Piper's Island, a good place for picnics."

Cory steered past a string of stones whose points tipped the surface in a line running out from the shore, into a section of the lake bordered by a mix of birch and maples. A web of lily pads spread out from the mouth of a small stream that fed into the lake. Cory killed the engine and let them drift toward shore. The sudden absence of the motor made the silence throb against Tyra's ears.

"This is my secret fishing spot," Cory said. "Sometimes the guests at the lodge pay me to guide them to fishing holes around the lake, but I save this one just for me."

It made Tyra smile to know that someone in Spirit Lake was willing to share something so special with her.

The front of the boat bumped against the shore. Cory hopped off and tied the bow line to a tree. Tyra jumped ashore and followed him as he walked into the woods.

"From the map, it looked like one of the Xs was close to the creek," Cory said.

Tyra remembered the thin blue line and a series of three *X*s and one box. But the map was so different from the actual forest, with trees and rocks everywhere. She hurried to keep up with Cory, who led them into a meadow lined with birch trees.

The wind made the leaves whisper and click against each other. The faint shushing of a small waterfall came through the trees, as the creek wandered down from the hill in front of them.

"We need to find some sign that he's been here," Tyra said. "If he's burying something, maybe he left a pile of dirt."

They searched the meadow but found no tell-tale signs. Near a cluster of rocks, Tyra discovered the rusty blade of a broken shovel.

"Look at this," Tyra said. "Someone was digging here, a long time ago."

"We need to see that map again."

The thought of sneaking another peek at Grandpa Rudy's precious maps sent a double shiver of fear and excitement through Tyra. "We can't let him suspect us," she said.

"Right. If we're going to tell him you went fishing, you'd better catch one," Cory said.

They returned to the boat and drifted toward the middle of the cove. Cory reached down for two fishing rods.

He showed her how to flip open the reel and hold the line with her finger while she cast, making sure the rod was pointing where she wanted the lure to go. They sat at opposite ends of the boat and lazily cast along the edge of the lily pads.

She and Cory spoke about their families and school. Neither of them had any brothers or sisters. Cory lived in Portsmouth, New Hampshire, and loved math but hated reading, the opposite of Tyra. He lived with his mother, who worked as a waitress. His father had moved to Colorado, with a new wife and new kids. Cory only got to talk to him a couple of times a year.

Tyra told him about living in Roxbury, deciding to focus on the good things, about her friends and the ice cream truck and Mrs. Starling, and about the history and stories that were part of everything, even the names of the streets. She decided not to mention the scary things that happened there sometimes.

"I don't really know any black people," Cory said. "We have two black kids at my school, but they're not in my grade. I never see anyone black up here. What's it like?"

Tyra wasn't sure what to say. "It's not like anything. It's just me. At my school, there aren't any white kids. A couple are mixed, though, so they're real light. In my neighborhood, we have all colors. What's it like being white?"

But she knew there was more to it than that. She knew why the men had stared at her in the store yesterday. And she knew that her white parents had chosen to live in Roxbury instead of other places, and part of the reason was that she was black. "Up here, I feel like I stand out. And not in a good way," she added.

Cory fidgeted with his fingers, making little diamond shapes, until he was suddenly interrupted by a splash near the edge of the lily pads. The line on Tyra's rod snaked through the water. "Pull up the tip!" he shouted and jumped over the seat toward her. He put his hands over hers and yanked the tip of the rod back into the air. "You've got a bite!"

Now that the hook was set and the reel engaged, Tyra could feel the fish pulling hard against the line. "What should I do?"

"Stay calm. He's a big one. Look at him run! Don't do anything yet, just hang tight. Keep the tip of your rod up. Don't let go, whatever you do." The rod flexed closer to the surface of the water, as the fish reversed direction and swam toward shore.

"Take up the slack. That's it. Good. Pull back a little. Keep tension on the line. You're doing great. He's a fighter."

Whenever the fish relaxed, Cory had her wind in the line a little more. After what seemed like hours, she pulled the fish all the way to the edge of the boat. Cory hooted. "It's a pike! And a beauty." With a quick motion, he grabbed a long-handled net and scooped the fish up into the air.

The pike was a brown-and-green tube of muscles and teeth, so long that its snout and eyes stuck out of the net as Cory hoisted it into the boat. Even though it was exhausted, the fish flexed its tail back and forth, trying to leap out of the net. Its teeth were sharp as needles. Tyra stared down at it, amazed she'd actually caught a fish. It stared back at her with a flat, glassy eye.

"What do we do now?" she asked.

"It's up to you," Cory answered. "Pike take extra work to clean, so I usually let them go. Plus, that way I can catch them again. But we can keep him if you want. I'm sure your grandfather would be impressed."

Tyra looked down at the fish. He'd fought so hard, and now they'd yanked him out of his home, away from his family. She knew how that felt. And she was still mad at Grandpa Rudy for not sticking up for her at the store and for not sharing his secrets. She didn't want to give him a glance at this beautiful creature. This one was just for her and Cory.

"Let him go," she said.

Cory smiled and unhooked the fish from the lure. He asked Tyra to grab a tape measure from his tackle box so they could measure the fish. Thirty-two inches. It filled both arms as Cory raised it over the edge of the boat, and before he could even set the fish in the water, it slapped its tail against Cory's hands, splashed into the lake, and disappeared.

#

Grandpa Rudy was waiting for them at the end of the dock, his mouth clenched tight in anger. His lips barely parted to make way for his voice. "Unacceptable."

Tyra knew she'd made a mistake, but she wasn't sorry. Not yet, anyway. "You were sound asleep. Snoring. I didn't want to—"

"No matter how much you don't like it, you're my responsibility now. You can't just run off without telling anyone. I didn't know what happened to you. You never know who might be around, watching, spying. I went searching for you."

"I didn't think you'd care," Tyra said in a small voice as she stepped onto the dock and stared at her sneakers.

His frown deepened, and he looked a little hurt. "Humph. While we're on the subject of responsibility, you're going to have to start pulling your weight around here. And you," he pointed to Cory, "your grandmother will have something to say about this."

"Oh, man. I gotta go. Bye, Tyra." Cory looked worried as he started the motor and drove away.

"Come with me." Grandpa Rudy led her to the barn. "You're going to have chores every morning, plus at some point the barn needs scraping and painting. First, though, I have a whole herd of tools that need cleaning and sharpening."

A collection of shovels, picks, and metal bars leaned against the workbench next to a neat assortment of files and a wire brush.

"You two were looking at my maps," he said as they entered the barn.

"What maps?"

"Don't play dumb with me. I left them on the workbench, but when I came in here, the tube was in the cart."

"But we didn't put it in the cart," Tyra said. "Honest!" She remembered clearly that they had left it on the workbench, just to the right of the lamps.

"I'm sure you're curious, but stay away from them. Got it?"

Tyra shrugged.

Grandpa Rudy picked up one of the files from the workbench. "This is called a bastard file. First you clamp the tool into the vise, and then you start filing. I'll show you how."

Tyra listened to his instructions, but she couldn't help wondering: *who had put the maps in the cart?*

#

Tyra's hands and arms ached, and she was covered with dirt and metal filings. The results of her afternoon's work hung on pegs along the wall by the workbench, the blades of the tools sharp and gleaming. They'd make perfect weapons in the hands of a maniac.

She only had one last mattock to sharpen, and she hoped Grandpa Rudy wouldn't come back with any more tools. She'd been working for hours and hours, with only a PB&J sandwich, some chips, and a banana for lunch. She never had to work this hard at home. It was completely and totally unfair.

She tightened the vise with a twist and pulled the file back toward her against the flat end of the tool, at an angle, as she'd been instructed. She was supposed to do a hundred strokes on each blade, and she knew he would check each tool. If it wasn't sharp, she'd have to do it again. *Scrape, scrape, scrape.*

Grandpa Rudy appeared at the door to the barn, but instead of more tools, he'd brought Lily. She crossed her arms and nodded approvingly.

"You should see what I've got Cory doing. He won't steer you into trouble again, I promise you that," she said.

Were all the grown-ups at Spirit Lake so tough?

"I was sorry to hear about your grandmother," Lily continued. "You must be awful worried about her. I'd like you and Rudy to come to the lodge for dinner tonight. This poor girl deserves a decent meal, after all this work, Rudy. And you probably could use a break from your own cooking."

"You've never tasted my cooking," Grandpa Rudy answered, meekly.

"You can't blame me for your bad manners. But I have a hunch. You'll be there tonight, right?"

Grandpa Rudy scuffed the toe of his boot in the dirt. "Well, I guess we could. I'd hate to impose."

"Excellent. We eat at six-thirty. We have our hands full with this man, don't we, Tyra? But we'll get through to him somehow. And now he's got you sharpening his digging tools. Rudy, you're turning your granddaughter into an accomplice. Tyra, you'd better be sure he's willing to share."

Lily winked at Tyra and turned on her heel back toward the dock. Grandpa Rudy jogged after her to catch up. "Now, Lily, you need to stop spreading rumors." They disappeared around the corner.

Accomplice! Share what? What did Lily know? Tyra desperately hoped dinner at the lodge would reveal some answers.

Chapter Seven

Tyra bounced out of her room, freshly showered and wearing a clean white polo shirt and navy-blue shorts. She was going to spend an evening with people who didn't mostly growl and scowl at her. Lily made her laugh, and Cory was already starting to feel like a real friend, even though he was a boy. If the lodge had Internet, she could email Déjà and Adriana. She stopped abruptly when she got to the back porch. Grandpa Rudy was sitting at the table, gazing out at the lake, still dressed in his dirty work clothes.

"Don't we need to go?" Tyra asked, desperately hoping dinner had not been canceled.

He kept staring out at the water. "I changed my mind."

"But..." Tyra couldn't believe it. He was going to ruin her one chance to have dinner with her only friend in Spirit Lake, with people who were actually nice, who might be good cooks. "Why?"

"It's complicated."

Was he embarrassed to be seen with her? Were the men from the store going to be there, and would they stare and make racial remarks? Maybe it wasn't worth it. But she couldn't spend another silent night at the cabin. She'd risk it, one more time. "Cory's my friend. And they're expecting us."

"You can go without me. You know how to drive the boat." He stood slowly, stiffly, like her dad did when he'd been working too hard at the community garden.

"You want me to drive all by myself?" Through the porch window, the lake stretched in front of them like a giant, scary ocean.

"You did pretty well the other day. As long as you drive straight, you'll be fine. Your dad could drive a boat by the time he was six years old. You think Cory is a water rat—you should've seen your dad. There was one summer, his feet never actually touched land. Come on, I'll help you get the motor started."

He walked her down to the lake, and she felt more and more nervous. What if she hit a rock and sank? The skies were clear and blue now, but what if a sudden storm sprang up and swamped her?

On the edge of the dock sat a bucket full of raspberries. After starting the motor and helping Tyra aboard, Grandpa Rudy handed her the bucket. "Take these to Lily."

Could it be that Grandpa Rudy was afraid to see Lily because he liked her? Boys at school got all weird when they liked a girl. Maybe they never changed, even when they were old and cranky like Grandpa Rudy. Tyra hid her smile. "That's very sweet."

His cheeks reddened. "Just tell her I . . . Oh, never mind. But ignore all the crazy things those people say. Half of it is lies, and the rest isn't true."

#

Nothing disastrous happened as Tyra pulled the boat away from the dock. The throttle felt awkward in her hand, but she gave it a twist and surged forward. The air pressed against her face, and she couldn't help smiling. She was driving—by herself! Nothing had ever made her feel so grown up. She felt like she could drive to the moon. Leaning her head back, she howled into the wind, "Yeeeehaaaa!"

When she reached the other side of the lake, Cory was waiting for her at the dock in front of the lodge. Her excitement at driving alone suddenly vanished. She eased off on the throttle, but the boat kept moving toward the dock. Was she going to crash? Right in front of Cory?

"Put it into reverse!" Cory shouted.

Reverse? How did that work? She couldn't remember. There was a switch or lever somewhere on the motor. Where? Her fingers found a small lever on the side. She clicked it back. The motor purred in neutral, but she was still moving forward. The dock was still getting closer. Boat don't have brakes. Why didn't boats have brakes?

"One more notch!" shouted Cory. She pressed the lever back again, and the motor shifted from neutral into reverse, growling and gurgling as the propeller pushed back against the water. The boat slowed quickly, and the wake she'd been trailing almost slopped over the stern. But the boat was stopping. Cory reached out and grabbed the nose right before it hit the dock, as the motor started to pull the craft backward. "Just shut it off," Cory said. "Twist the throttle off."

Tyra did, and all was quiet. Her heart was beating like crazy, but she had managed not to crash. Barely.

Cory tied the bow line to the dock. "Not too bad for your first landing," he said. "It's easy, once you get the hang of it. We can practice after dinner. Where's your grandfather?"

"He couldn't come."

"I'm glad he let you drive here alone."

"I think he felt guilty about staying home."

"It's a good thing you're here," Cory said. "Because the only kids staying at the lodge now are babies and little kids, or else teenagers who never say anything and sneak out in the canoes to smoke cigarettes. Did your grandfather make you work real hard?"

She showed him her red palms, and they traded chore horror stories. Cory had spent all afternoon scrubbing old ashes and grease from barbecue grill grates.

"Do you think he'll go out digging for treasure again tonight?" Cory asked. "Maybe he's out there right now."

"Something weird happened. He asked if we'd been looking at the maps."

"Did you confess?"

"No. But when he found the maps, they weren't where we'd left them."

"Are you sure?"

"We left them on the bench, by the lamps, but he said they were in the wheelbarrow. What if someone besides us was snooping around?"

"Whatever he's after must be valuable," Cory said. "Come on, we can think about it at dinner. I'm starving." Even though he was sore from chores, he still had enough energy to do cartwheels all the way down the dock. Tyra attempted one of her own, right behind him, then ran back for the bucket of berries.

The varnished logs making up the beams and walls filled the lodge's lobby with warm light. The chairs and couches and railings were made from branches and tree trunks. It was like being inside the skeleton of a forest. A fireplace made of mossy rocks opened wide on the back wall, and the chimney climbed high into the rafters. A taxidermy moose head with broad antlers and a serious expression hung on one wall. A stuffed black bear reared up in a corner.

"Wow," Tyra said.

"I knew you'd like this room," Cory said. "This lodge was built a zillion years ago, when movie stars used to come up here for the summer."

Tyra noticed a desk in the corner with a computer. "Could I send an email to my friends in Boston? I bet they're worried about me."

"Sure." He showed her how to log on, then waited patiently, which for Cory meant attempting to balance a ruler on his chin while ignoring his growling stomach.

More than a dozen messages from Adriana and Déjà were waiting. Her friends were doing exactly what Tyra had expected: eating ice cream, swimming at the pool, watching Adriana's little sister, hanging out. And wondering what happened to Tyra.

Subject: Where R U???

Tyra, where you at?? Have the bears eaten you?! Mom says if you was eaten by bears we would see it on the news. Maybe you got lost in the woods. Adriana said maybe you found all new friends. This is message number ten we sent.

OOOO xxxxxx
Déjà (ur sistah)

Even in the grand lodge, with the light of the sunset bathing everything in gold, Tyra missed her friends and her neighborhood. Although people were sometimes afraid to go there, Roxbury had its own sunsets, ones that made the tower on the hill glow orange and pink, like a castle out of a fairy tale. She quickly typed a message to her friends.

Subject: Still alive!

Hi Déjà!! Hi Adriana!! I'm still alive, but I miss you both, a ton. My grandma smashed her elbow in Mexico, so I have to spend all summer at my grandpa's cabin. Grandpa Rudy doesn't have a computer, not even a TV!!!! This will probably be the worst summer ever. Mean people. Chores. Torture. Got in trouble for going fishing with Cory, a kid who lives here. Everyone here has to work all the time, especially if you get in trouble. People are even tougher than your mom, Déjà (but not louder).

My grandfather is up to something mysterious out in the woods. But I don't know what yet. Am determined to find out.

You keep having fun while I suffer. Wish I was there. Eat some ice cream for me.

Love, Tyra

#

Cory led Tyra to the dining room, where two long tables sat end to end under a high ceiling crisscrossed with beams made of peeled logs. A wall of glass looked out over the lake with a view like something on a poster or magazine cover. Lodge guests occupied most of the seats around the tables, and the happy sound of their chatter filled the room, in a way that reminded Tyra of neighborhood barbecues back home. On the back wall of the dining room hung framed black-and-white photographs from Spirit Lake's past: picnics in front of the lodge, a smiling man standing beside a fancy old car with his son perched on the hood, a castle made of blocks of ice, men proudly displaying a string of fish they'd caught.

Lily came out of the kitchen carrying a dish of lasagna, and her face lit up with welcome at the sight of Tyra. "I'm so glad you made it. Where's your grandfather?"

"He decided not to come."

Lily pursed her lips. "Hm. I still have hope in my heart that he won't stay a hermit forever. How did your dad turn out to be so well socialized with a father like Rudy?"

"He sent you these. I think he picked them himself." Tyra held out the bucket of raspberries.

Lily smiled and clucked with surprise. "I do have a special place in my heart for raspberries. Your grandfather is the king of mixed messages. Cory, take these into the kitchen, please. Tyra, come sit down here with us."

Lily introduced her to the lodge guests. Ted was there, his face sunburned from a day on the lake. He wore a striped dress shirt, and without his fishing lure–covered hat and vest, Tyra barely recognized him. Next to Ted sat a honeymooning couple, Tim and Becky, who cuddled so close to each other they could have used just one chair. Across the table was Meredith, from New Orleans, who came to Spirit Lake Lodge year after year because summer in the Louisiana heat was too much for someone with her delicate constitution. She wore a flowing green dress of gauzy fabric and lots of dangly bracelets and beads. Beside Meredith sat Walter, a bear of a man, with a dark beard and hairy arms and little crinkles near the corners of his eyes that went with his booming laugh.

No one stared at Tyra, but instead they all busily ate, passing the lasagna, rolls, peas and carrots, and salad, and told stories from the day—about fishing, getting lost in the wrong cove, or tipping over the sailboat. The honeymooners mostly exchanged loving smiles.

"Tyra caught a pike today," Cory bragged. "Thirty-two inches. Her first fish ever!"

"Very impressive. How about you, Ted? Almost catch your whopper again?" teased Walter.

"Must have been seven pounds if it was an ounce," Ted answered, mopping his brow with a napkin. His bright-green eyes lit up when he smiled. "Just about snapped my rod. He jumped out of the water and spit that lure back at me so hard that the hook lodged into the seat. Next time I'll set the hook better. That new Rapala lure is going to be my secret weapon."

"That fish is probably down at the bottom of the lake right now, telling the story to all his friends. Or to a ghost. This lake isn't called Spirit Lake for nothing," said Walter through a mouthful of potatoes.

"Maybe to the ghost of Emerald Eddie," said Ted.

"Who's Emerald Eddie?" asked Tyra.

"The ghost of a gangster," replied Walter.

"Oh, Walter," said Lily. "Don't get started."

"A real gangster?" asked Tyra, her eyes growing wide.

"He certainly was. And he used to spend his summers at Spirit Lake," Walter continued, shifting forward on his seat toward Tyra and Cory. "Emerald Eddie McCoy was a gangster in the Roaring Twenties, a bootlegger, back in the days of Prohibition. There was a fortune to be made smuggling whiskey and beer and rum across the Canadian border. He owned a cottage on the shore, down near your grandfather's place, Tyra. It burned down years ago. Some people think there was another cabin, a secret one. No one knows where. They say that's where his treasure is buried." The table grew quiet.

"Emerald Eddie was almost as famous as Al Capone and even more ruthless. He always wore an emerald ring and an emerald lapel pin. He liked the way it brought out the color of his eyes. He even drove a green Cadillac, a nineteen twenty-eight 341A Town Sedan. One of the most beautiful cars ever made. That's him and his car on the wall, over there, with his son."

Walter pointed his thick finger at the photo Tyra had seen earlier, and they turned to stare at the man with the fedora and wide, confident smile, standing with his foot on the running board.

"The law was hot on his trail, but he was too smart for them. Then one day, the G-men—that's the government cops—got the jump on him when he was on his way to Canada with a safe full of cash and gems. He knew the back roads that could get him secretly across the border, but the police cut him off. He ditched the car somewhere near his secret cabin and had his goons bury the safe in the woods. Some say he killed them, to guarantee the secret would never be revealed."

"What happened to him?" Tyra asked.

"He tried to escape by boat, but the police caught up with him. There was a big shoot-out on the water, out past Piper's Island. Emerald Eddie didn't go without a fight, but finally, it was over—the gangster and his boat were full of holes. His body slipped into the water and disappeared into the dark depths of Spirit Lake, never to be found.

"No one else knew where the safe was buried, and no one has ever found it, or the cabin, or even the car. There are miles and miles of shoreline and woods around this lake. When Emerald Eddie died, the secret of his treasure died with him."

Walter leaned in toward Tyra and Cory, his voice barely a whisper. "Some people say he still haunts the rocks along the far shore, ready to pull anyone in who gets too close to his treasure."

The dining room was eerily silent. Suddenly, Lily clapped her hands together, and everyone jumped and laughed. "Walter, you're scaring the children. This is a story for the dark of night by the campfire, with no little ears listening. Everyone in Spirit Lake goes through an Emerald Eddie phase, digging in the woods. Usually takes about two holes for them to realize there's nothing but dirt and rocks in the ground up here. Even your dad dug a few, Tyra."

"My dad?" Tyra's dad spent his whole life trying to be different from Spirit Lake. She liked imagining him digging for buried treasure.

"Our parents aren't always what they seem, honey. But like most people, your dad outgrew his digging phase. Unfortunately, some folks never do. Now, who wants some fresh raspberries and whipped cream?"

The buzz of conversation rose again, starting with Emerald Eddie, but quickly moving on to the weather and plans for tomorrow.

Tyra and Cory couldn't take their eyes from Walter.

"Is that all true?" Tyra asked.

"Absolutely," Walter said.

Tyra took one last bite of lasagna. Everything was much clearer now.

Cory leaned toward her and whispered, "I think someone is still looking for that treasure."

Tyra nodded. "My Grandpa Rudy."

Chapter Eight

After dessert, the guests gathered around a raging bonfire in the stone-lined fire ring on the beach, and Walter told more ghost stories, changing his voice and twisting his body to play each character. Besides gangsters, over the years the lake had filled with the restless spirits of jilted lovers, lost ice fishermen, tipsy teenagers, and more. When Tyra looked out at the lake, she imagined she could see the water bubbling from all the lost souls trapped below.

She tried to shake off the creepiness by looking up at the sky, where the stars shone brighter than she'd ever seen before. A crescent moon was rising behind the black shadows of the mountains.

"You'd better get home before your grandfather thinks we've decided to keep you for good," said Lily.

"Maybe we can go fishing again tomorrow," Cory said, through bites of a gooey roasted marshmallow.

"I'd like that." Tyra wished the night would just flow into morning, that they could eat marshmallows until it was time to go fishing, and that summer would ease on ahead, one smiling minute after another. She didn't want to move from this spot— especially not to cross the lake again, all by herself. After Walter's stories, the last place she wanted to be was alone on the dark water.

They walked Tyra down to the dock, and Lily handed her a flashlight. "I don't know why Rudy didn't give you something to help you see your way home. I swear that man can't think of anything besides that ridiculous treasure."

Tyra thought that Lily was as much of a distraction to Grandpa Rudy as Emerald Eddie's loot, but she didn't say so. Instead, she climbed into the boat and pulled the starter cord. Nothing happened. She pulled again, harder this time, and the engine sputtered to life. Cory and Lily untied the ropes.

"Are you sure you'll be all right?" Lily asked.

Tyra was determined to be tough, although the waves against the hull sounded a little too much like the tapping of skeletal fingers. "I'll be fine."

Lily pointed across the lake to a solitary bright speck in the middle of a black shore. "At least he put on a light for you. Don't worry, just stay pointed at that light—there are no rocks or snags between here and there. You'll be home in no time. And tell Rudy thanks for the raspberries."

Tyra steered out onto the lake, and soon Cory, Lily, and the lodge were far behind her. She gripped the tiller stick tightly, pointing the flashlight out into the night. Its thin beam was swallowed by the darkness pressing against her, and she tried not to look too closely at the water, afraid she might see ghostly hands and faces beneath the surface. She ran the motor as fast as it would go, leaning into the wind, her braids streaming off her shoulders, willing the journey to be over.

And suddenly it was. Grandpa Rudy had lined up a dozen camping lanterns on the dock, brightly welcoming her home. This time, she slowed down long before she got to the landing and barely had to reverse the engine. She turned off the motor and drifted to the dock with just a light bump.

Tyra climbed out of the boat and picked up one of the lanterns. The path between the dock and the house was dark and scary. The woods were full of rustling noises. Did the ghosts of Spirit Lake ever leave the water and haunt the forest, too? Was Grandpa Rudy already out in the woods looking for Emerald Eddie's buried loot? What would it take to get him to turn away from that treasure and notice the people right in front of him?

Grandpa Rudy was sitting on the worn plaid couch in the living room, looking at a leather-bound photo album. His reading glasses perched low on his nose, and his eyes looked sad and old behind them. Tyra sat down next to him before he even noticed she was there. He startled and gently closed the album.

Tyra reached out and opened it again. Inside was a photo of a young couple—a tall, athletic woman with a small boy on her hip, next to a muscular man with a huge smile. He was pointing to a stone foundation that Tyra recognized as the base for the cabin.

"That's you," Tyra said.

"And your dad. And Grandma Betty."

They looked at the photo in silence for a while, and then Tyra turned the pages to see more photos of the young family, with friends and relatives, and the cabin gradually rising to completion.

"I wish I'd known her."

"You would've liked her. She would've known what to do with you."

"Thank you for showing me how to handle the boat."

"Did you enjoy your dinner at the lodge?"

Tyra nodded. "Do you still miss her?"

"More than I should. It's been a long, long time, and it still feels like I just lost her yesterday. I do what I can to keep my mind off her. It's hard to explain to someone so young."

Tyra turned the page to a photo of Grandma Betty standing in the kitchen, wagging a finger at the photographer.

"Sometimes," Tyra said, "I miss my birth parents, and I never even met them. I don't know much about them, but there's a tiny empty space inside me. Even when there are people all around me and they're being kind and saying nice things, I still feel it. I think the way you feel about Grandma Betty makes sense."

Tyra had never told anyone how it felt to miss her birth parents, not even her mom or dad, but it felt all right to tell Grandpa Rudy. Especially the version of her grandfather with sad eyes sitting next to her right now. He understood about missing people and about secrets.

"I think we both make plenty of sense," he said gently.

They turned through more pages, until they came to a photo of a whole bunch of people in front of Spirit Lake Lodge, which looked the same as it did today, just a little newer. Grandpa Rudy and Grandma Betty and Tyra's dad stood beside another family, a compact blonde woman posing for the camera with her husband and daughter. They looked like they were having the best summer day ever. Tyra instantly recognized the blonde woman's hands-on-hips, no-nonsense stance. "That's Lily, isn't it? Did her husband die, too?"

"Yes. We had some tough years around this lake." Grandpa Rudy's expression was a mix of the happy remembrance of that day and the hard times that followed.

"Lily really liked the berries you sent."

Which was the wrong thing to say. Grandpa Rudy snapped the album shut. "That's enough for tonight," he growled. "It's late. You need to get to bed."

Chapter Nine

Subject: What's he digging for?

Hi Adriana and Déjà!

It's been more than a week, and I haven't been eaten by bears yet. I did see a moose this morning when Cory and I went fishing. Moose are huge! Taller than Kelvin Morrison, and with legs just as long and bony. Adriana, you would've screamed.

Be glad you're not here. Every morning I have a whole list of chores.

Cory caught a lake trout yesterday, number 10 on his list (of 15). He was so excited that he jumped into the lake and swam laps around the boat. One day we just sat in the boat and waited to see how far the wind would blow us. Miles. It sounds boring, but it was actually fun. (Déjà—I know he's a boy, but you read too many of your sister's romance novels.)

I snuck a look at a bunch of history books on Grandpa Rudy's shelves. Emerald Eddie was real! I think Grandpa's digging for his treasure every night, but I don't know for sure. I have a plan. If you don't hear from me again, then my plan failed in a really bad way.

The knife you gave me will come in handy.

Wish you were here. (Swimming in a lake isn't so bad.)

Xxxx oooooo
Ur country sistah, Tyra

#

Tyra lay still under the covers and breathed deeply, pretending to be asleep when Grandpa Rudy cracked the door open for his nightly check before heading out to the barn. As soon as he closed the door, she flung off the covers. Then she padded down the hall and slipped out onto the porch, watching from the shadows as Grandpa Rudy pushed the cart onto the path.

This time, she was prepared. She wore long sleeves and jeans and had sprayed herself with bug spray to keep the mosquitoes away. She brought the flashlight that Lily had loaned her. Now she wouldn't trip over roots and could keep up with Grandpa Rudy. And she even had a plan to keep from getting lost: she would use the pocketknife from Adriana and Déjà to cut blazes onto tree trunks to mark her path, as Grandpa Rudy led her deeper and deeper into the woods.

Up ahead, Grandpa Rudy pushed the cart down the narrow path through the trees, around a gathering of boulders. His tools rattled and clanked so much that Tyra almost didn't have to worry about being quiet. She walked on her tiptoes anyway, just in case. If he caught her, she didn't know what he'd do.

#

Finally, Grandpa Rudy stopped near a small clearing. Tyra crouched behind a big rock. The thought of spiders and bugs crawling around in the dark made her itchy.

Grandpa Rudy pulled out a lantern and laid a board between two rocks, forming a makeshift desk. He spread out his maps and, after careful study, walked over to a thick tree trunk and took eleven paces. He scratched a mark on the ground with his boot. With a pick and shovel, he traced a big square in the dirt and began to dig. Occasionally, when a tree creaked in the breeze or an animal made a noise, he would jerk his head up, eyes wide, peering into the shadows.

How many nights had he spent out in the woods? How many years had he been looking? What would he do with all that treasure if he found it? So many nights in the dark, digging and digging and digging.

Tyra leaned back against the rock, wondering how long they'd be out here tonight.

#

The lantern shone brightly on Tyra's face, jolting her awake. She struggled to jump to her feet, but Grandpa Rudy had a tight grip on her arm. He leaned his face close to hers.

"Who set you up to this? Why aren't you asleep in bed? You have no right to be out here. I should've known you couldn't be trusted."

Tyra could barely open her mouth to speak. Over Grandpa Rudy's shoulder, she could see a broad, shallow hole, with rocks scattered around the edges. No treasure chest.

"Are you looking for Emerald Eddie's treasure?"

His eyes narrowed suspiciously. "Who said anything about Emerald Eddie? I don't know what you're talking about. And neither do you. It's none of your business, anyway. Don't breathe a word about this. You could bring grave danger to us. Understand?"

She nodded, with a gulp. "But it's not a secret. Everyone knows about Emerald Eddie. They were talking about him at dinner."

"People say all kinds of things. Am I a crazy old man? You'd better believe it. And you're a disobedient brat. Do I need to lock you up at night? You will not ruin this for me. I have been searching for too long. I'm so close."

"How do you know?"

"I just know."

"But what if you never find it?"

That was not a question he wanted to hear. If it were possible, the look in his eyes might have set her on fire and burned her to a crisp.

"Enough. Let's go." He pulled Tyra by the arm all the way through the woods back to the cabin. He opened the door to her room and thrust her inside. "Go to bed. But first, you need to swear to keep this a secret."

"Okay."

"Really swear. Say, I, Tyra Palmer, swear never to tell anyone about Grandpa Rudy digging for treasure or where it is."

She raised her right hand. "I, Tyra Palmer, swear never to tell anyone about Grandpa Rudy digging for treasure or where it is. But everyone already knows anyway."

"They don't know what they know, and neither do you. Get some sleep." He slammed the door and Tyra watched through the window as he trudged back into the woods. The sky was turning from black to blue.

#

Tyra and Grandpa Rudy ate their breakfast cereal in silence, the sun already heating up the day. When Tyra broke into an enormous yawn, Grandpa Rudy looked up. "You need to get more rest. Don't worry, when you're finished today, you won't have any trouble sleeping all night long."

After breakfast, Grandpa Rudy brought her outside and handed Tyra a metal-bladed paint scraper and pointed at the side of the barn, with its pastures of peeling red paint. "Start in this corner and work your way around the entire barn."

Tyra scraped and scraped and scraped. She scraped up and down; she scraped from side to side. She reached to scrape high above her head, and she scraped while kneeling on the ground. From time to time, Grandpa Rudy would return to point out any spots she'd missed and refill her thermos with ice water. When she finished the first long side of the barn, he came back with a ladder and scraped above where she'd been working, up to the roofline.

Would her mother and father fly home from France if they knew she was being forced to do all this work? Did her father know that Grandpa Rudy spent every night in the woods digging holes? She'd finally talked to her parents a few nights ago, when she'd been happy after a day of fishing and skipping rocks with Cory. They were relieved to hear that she had a friend. Her mom said Paris was very romantic, with its cathedrals and the narrow streets of Montmartre. They sounded happy—which was good, because she really wanted them to stay married. But it wasn't fair for them to get to have fun while she was stuck doing slave labor for a crazy old man who constantly thought about ghosts and treasure. In the fall, her teacher would ask, "How did you spend your summer vacation?" and she would have to answer, "Being tortured. Scraping paint off the world's biggest barn." This was not how summer vacations were supposed to be.

Grandpa Rudy brought her a tuna salad sandwich, a pickle, and potato chips for lunch in the shade, then she was back to scraping. She'd just started on one of the short ends of the barn when she heard the motor of Cory's boat. She dropped her scraper and ran around the corner, just in time to see Grandpa Rudy intercept Cory at the end of the dock. She walked toward them, hoping she'd served her sentence and would be released from Camp Work-Till-You-Drop.

"Tyra's busy today. And tomorrow, too. She's earned herself some extra chores."

Cory poked his tanned face around Grandpa Rudy to give Tyra a smile before he retreated to his boat.

"That's not fair," Tyra protested. "I have to be able to have *some* fun. My mom and dad didn't leave me here for this. There are agencies who frown on this sort of thing."

"I don't think a few days of chores constitutes child abuse," Grandpa Rudy said as he escorted her back to the barn and handed her the scraper. "Keep it up. You're doing a good job."

#

That night, after a long shower to wash off the dust and paint scrapings, Tyra lay in bed staring at the blisters on her hands. She was almost too tired to admire her own misery.

The sound of a drill came from outside her door. A squeal of metal into wood. "Grandpa?"

"I'm screwing the door shut, so you stay put."

"You can't board me up in here."

"You've proven you can't be trusted. It's too dangerous to have you traipsing through the woods at night."

"What if there's a fire?"

"The drop out the window is only a few feet. Oh, and I put a bucket in the corner, in case nature calls."

In a moment, she saw him in the dark by the freshly scraped barn, gathering his tools. He looked up at her grimly and vanished into the night.

Chapter Ten

"Psst."

Tyra looked up from her paint scraping. Over the past two days, she'd worked three quarters of the way around the barn, leaving the exposed siding behind her a silvery gray. Grandpa Rudy spent the whole second day up on a ladder, scraping the higher spots. He was a relentless worker and had already caught up and passed her. But today he'd gone off in the boat. He wouldn't say where, but Tyra was sure it had to do with the treasure.

"Psst. Over here." Cory crawled through the tall grass and milkweed behind the barn and poked his head out.

"What are you doing?" Tyra had never been so glad to see anyone in her life.

"Your grandfather is at the lodge, helping my grandma fix the roof of one of the cabins."

"Really?"

"She's busy talking at him; he's busy not saying much of anything. It could take a while. I told them I was going fishing."

Cory crawled the rest of the way out of the woods. He was always trying different things with his body—he'd stand on one foot for ten minutes or hang upside down from a branch, just to see how it felt. "I'm here to rescue you," he said.

"I need it. When he goes out treasure hunting at night, he screws my door shut."

"What if he got eaten by a pack of coyotes while he was out in the woods?"

"I'd waste away. They'd find my dried-up skeleton."

Cory shook his head. "That's twisted. You need to get away."

"If I don't finish, I'll get in more trouble."

"You've already had two days of chores with no adventures. You might die if you don't get a break."

Tyra could be satisfied with finding some of her adventures in the books she read, but Cory wanted his thrills in person or not at all.

"Is he starving you? I brought some apples and potato salad, just in case."

"He left me lunch inside—some sandwiches and chips and cookies."

"Maybe they're drugged, to remove your initiative. My grandmother says I have too much initiative, except when it's time for chores. Anyway, he won't be back until after lunch. Let's go."

"I don't know." Tyra really, really, really wanted to go. But the prospect of getting into more trouble with Grandpa Rudy terrified her.

"We'll be back in time," Cory reassured her. "Look, I'll help you scrape. We'll scrape at double speed for twenty minutes. With two of us doing it, we'll do four times as much. When he gets home, it'll look like you made all this progress." Enamored with his new plan, Cory attacked the wall of the barn with a scraper. Despite how tired she was, Tyra did her best to move at double speed.

After a while, they stepped back and admired the results. Not perfect, but it looked like someone had worked hard for a long time. Hard enough. Tyra rushed into the kitchen to stuff the lunch into a bag, then they ran off into the woods.

#

Once they were away from the barn, time resumed its proper summer pace. Tyra and Cory pushed through dense pines into the cool glow of a birch glade. "Maybe Emerald Eddie walked right here, trying to decide where to bury his treasure," Tyra said.

Cory picked up a stick and held it like a machine gun. "This way, boys. No one will ever find it."

"Maybe he was being chased by ghosts from the lake." Tyra held out her arms in front of her like a zombie. "Oooooo. Oooooo, join us, Eddie. Come into the lake with us."

She chased Cory around the glade, weaving through the trees with their ghostly paper bark. They laughed and ran until it was necessary to eat sandwiches. As they searched for the exact right picnic rock, Cory spotted a scrape on the side of a maple tree.

"Hey, someone's been here."

Tyra looked at the tree. "I made that with my pocketknife, when I followed Grandpa Rudy into the woods." Tyra remembered her promise to never tell anyone about the digging, but that was before Grandpa Rudy screwed her door shut at night and made her scrape paint day after day. Plus, promises made under duress weren't as strong as regular promises. And Cory wasn't just anyone—he could be trusted.

"You followed him?"

"That's why I got in so much trouble. I fell asleep, and he found me. I made these marks so I could find my way home."

"Very smart." He rubbed his fingers on the cut tree bark. "So we could follow these back to the cabin. Or, if we walk in the other direction, they'll lead us to where he was digging."

The thought of going to the dig site made Tyra nervous, but she couldn't admit that to Cory. She led them deeper into the woods. The path twisted up and down and across the slope. Finally, they reached a small clearing. Four neat squares of raw dirt showed where Grandpa Rudy had dug holes and filled them back in again.

"So this could be the place, huh?" Cory picked up a handful of dirt and let it slip through his fingers.

Tyra noticed a fifth spot, a little way off from the other four. It wasn't a square, but sort of a squiggly circle. "Why didn't he make this one in the same shape?"

"Maybe he ran out of time," Cory suggested.

Tyra wasn't so sure. Grandpa Rudy had a method to his madness. This other spot looked more random. Could someone else be out there digging, too?

"Where were you hiding when he found you?" Cory asked.

"Behind this rock." Tyra led him to where she'd fallen asleep two nights ago. The flat-topped rock was also a good place for a picnic, so they unpacked their bologna sandwiches, chips, and cookies.

"How mad was he?" Cory asked.

"Like sparks were going to come shooting out of his ears." Tyra didn't mention that he'd also seemed a little afraid. What was he worried about?

"Nuclear. That's what I call it when my mom gets like that. My grandmother, she mostly gets quiet, and her voice gets that tone, you know, the one that feels real hard."

Tyra knew that tone very well from her own mother. "Do you think he'll ever find it?"

Cory had already finished his sandwich and was polishing off his chips. Even though he was skinny, Cory was famous all across Spirit Lake for being able to eat as much as any grown-up. Lily said that one day all that eating would catch up with him and he'd be seven feet tall.

"He's been looking for a long time," Tyra continued. "If he was going to find it, don't you think he would've by now?"

"That's the thing with treasure: once you stop looking, you won't find it, so you can never stop. Think of it—a safe filled with emeralds, diamonds, and gold." Cory examined a spot of ground between the four filled-in holes. "Maybe he should have dug here instead. If we come back with some shovels, we might find it."

"He would kill us."

"We'd share it with him. What would you do with millions of dollars?"

"I don't know. How about you?"

"I'd make it so my mom could quit her job. That way, she could come here in the summers with me. We could buy our own place on the lake, and I could hire someone to do my chores, so I could go fishing whenever I wanted. And I'd buy a new fishing boat, though not with sonar, because that's cheating. Or a wooden guideboat. They're so beautiful, even though you have to row them. If we lived up here all year long, I could go ice fishing."

Tyra had never known anyone who thought about fishing as much as Cory.

"If I had millions," she said, "I'd buy a bunch of airplane tickets, so I could visit my Grandma Feather in the hospital and fly to Paris to see my parents."

"You could buy your own plane and hire someone to fly it."

"Or I could learn to fly it myself. And I'd buy a new phone. And a house with a yard and a garden. Not a new house, but an old one that comes with stories and secret hidden stashes, so we could start a whole new treasure hunt. And I'd have an ice cream party for the whole neighborhood, and you could come, too."

"Do it at Fenway Park, so we can watch the Red Sox."

Tyra didn't care much about baseball, but she agreed to hold it at Fenway, for Cory's sake. A sound came from the woods—a branch snapping. Tyra and Cory froze. A sudden explosion of wings and feathers brushed past them as two grouse flushed from the edge of the clearing.

"Get down!" Cory hissed. They dove off the boulder and pressed against the ground. "Someone's out there."

They raised their heads above the rock and spied Grandpa Rudy creeping through the woods, carrying a pick handle at the ready, like a weapon. Like if he caught someone, he'd bash their skulls open. He stopped by the circular patch of dirt and prodded at the soil, puzzled.

"We have to get out of here," Tyra whispered.

"On the count of three," Cory answered. "Go as fast as you can, through the woods. Don't let him see us. *One. Two. Three!*"

On three, they ran away from Grandpa Rudy, faster than they'd ever run before, deeper into the forest. A shout echoed behind them.

Cory led the way, but Tyra kept up with him, even though her side was starting to hurt and her lungs burned. They ran and ran, over rocks and roots, through bushes, past stumps, and over fallen logs.

"Cory, stop. Let me catch my breath," Tyra panted. They stood for a moment, leaning against a towering tree. Vines climbed all the way around the trunk, and some even dangled from branches down to the ground, like in a Tarzan movie.

"Maybe we lost him," said Cory, as out of breath as Tyra.

From the woods came the snapping of more branches and the distant sound of Grandpa Rudy shouting, "Hey, you, whoever you are. Get off my property! This is my land. Get off my land!"

"He doesn't know it's us," Tyra said.

"He will if he catches us. Come on!"

So they ran again. The woods went on forever. Tyra and Cory skittered down a steep slope. They squished their way around the edge of a swampy bog full of butterflies and mosquitoes and came out the other side onto an overgrown road shaded by ancient oaks.

They listened for any sign that Grandpa Rudy was still following them. Nothing. Just the sound of birds and the buzzing of a bumblebee.

"I think we did it," Tyra said. "But we should keep moving. He can be sneaky."

Pushing through waist-high weeds, they wound their way down the abandoned road. After a few minutes, they lost the track altogether as it melted into the forest, but they pressed ahead, and it reappeared. In the woods off to the right, an old stone wall followed alongside the road until it finally petered out into random rocks. A speck of light ahead showed that they'd come close to the lake. The old road opened up into a clearing, lined with thick pine trees. Opposite the pines stood an enormous boulder, as big as a house, and a pile of smaller rocks, reaching higher than their heads, covering one whole side of the boulder.

They'd started walking through the clearing, when something caught Tyra's eye. On one side of the open area, across from the big boulder and rock pile, almost invisible behind bushes and fallen trees, an old log cabin leaned precariously to one side. It looked like it might collapse at any second.

"Whoa. Look at that," Tyra said.

"Let's go in."

"Is it safe?"

"Safer than being out here. He'll never find us in there. We almost walked right past it."

Inside the cabin, the floor creaked and groaned, and in places the boards had rotted through completely. Mounds of leaves, pine cones, twigs, and moss gathered in the corners, lit dimly by sun filtering through holes in the corrugated tin roof and missing logs in the walls. The windows clung to a few remaining shards of glass, but otherwise did nothing to stop the breeze blowing in off the lake. From the back window, they could see the water shimmering on the other side of a row of trees.

"Somebody's old hunting cabin," Cory said. "I've found a couple of them in the woods over by my grandma's place." He opened the door to an old woodstove in the corner and a stream of acorns poured out. "Guess the squirrels own it now."

Tyra stood by one of the windows, listening. "I don't hear him. Maybe we lost him."

"Did you see him with that pick handle?"

Tyra didn't know what to think. What if he found out they'd been at the site? How angry would he be? How it would feel if someone tried to take something of hers, something that she obsessed over? How would it feel if someone tried to take her bike, her phone, and all her books? But even then, it wouldn't be the same. He'd better not find out it was them.

In the corner, Cory poked through the leaves and found a green bottle that narrowed in the middle, almost like it had a waist, with deep ridges and embossed lettering reading *Vess Dry*. "Cool. Look at this. It's not even broken. And it looks super old."

Tyra went to a different corner and kicked aside some rubbish to reveal an ancient suitcase, its brown leather mostly replaced by black mold and moss. She felt an electric tingle up her spine. "What if this was Emerald Eddie's? This could be his secret cabin. Maybe his clothes are inside this suitcase, or maybe it has a map to the buried treasure."

"Maybe he put the money in the suitcase, because he was in such a hurry." Cory clearly liked the story as much as Tyra.

"Let's open it," she said.

Together they banged at the clasps until they finally released. With a deep breath, they opened the case.

The musty smell of mildewed cloth filled the air. Tyra reached in and pulled out clumped socks and old-fashioned underwear and men's shirts. Nothing remotely resembling gems or gold. And no map.

"Not exactly a treasure chest," Cory said with a sigh.

"But still, look how old it is. It did belong to someone from a long time ago."

"It smells."

Tyra rummaged around some more and found an old straight razor, its blade spotted with rust. She imagined Emerald Eddie shaving around the smug smile she'd seen in the photo at the lodge.

They poked around the rest of the cabin, under collapsed sections of the roof and rafters, and in a nest made by a raccoon or some other animal. They found two broken plates, some old tin silverware, and a mirror that looked like it had been ripped from the door of an ancient car.

"I'm keeping this," Cory said, holding up the green bottle. "It's like a message in a bottle, just without the message."

Tyra decided to keep the mirror. She could use it to spy around corners, to see when her grandfather was coming to check on her at the barn. Or she could use it to flash signals to Cory from across the lake. She liked the shape of it and how it had fought off the rust, despite years of lying under sticks and feathers and leaves.

"I'm hungry," Cory said.

Tyra pulled what was left of their lunch out of the bag. Luckily, she'd thought to grab it when they ran, or else Grandpa Rudy would have known for sure it was them at the dig site. They split the last sandwich, the potato salad, and an apple. When they were done, they put their new treasures, the mirror and the bottle, into the lunch bag and stepped cautiously outside the cabin.

"Do you know where we are?" asked Tyra.

"Not exactly. We were going so fast, I couldn't pay attention. And I don't know this side of the lake."

"So we're lost?" What if they had to stay out in the woods all night? What if they never found their way home? Walter's ghost stories started to burble at the back of her mind. If this was Emerald Eddie's cabin, did he haunt it in the dark?

"The good news is that the lake is right here," Cory said, as they walked to the water's edge. "It'll be slow, but we can follow the shore until we come to your grandpa's cabin. I anchored my boat near your place, so I can sneak home and you can slip back over to the barn. Maybe your grandfather won't even have missed you."

"He'll know."

"We can take my boat back to the lodge and tell my grandmother that your grandpa is crazy and locks you in at night. She'll let you stay with us."

Anything would be better than getting sealed in her room night after night and scraping paint day after day. Lily was always so nice, and she'd let them go fishing whenever they wanted, and Tyra could help out to earn her keep. Maybe Grandpa Rudy would be relieved to be rid of her, so he could dig without worrying whether she might steal his treasure. Tyra wished she could have a normal grandfather who liked her and wanted to do normal grandfather things.

#

Walking around the shore meant a constant climb over rocks and logs while they pushed through prickly bushes and avoided poison ivy, which made for a slow journey home. After what felt like hours, they came to a bend in the shoreline and a new expanse of water opened in front of them. No sign of houses or cabins, nor of Cory's boat. But not far from shore was a different boat—it was Ted, in his fishing vest and lure-covered hat, lazily casting toward an old log. His binoculars hung around his neck at the ready to spy on odd birds.

"What do you think?" Tyra asked.

"He'll give us a ride back to my boat. If we keep walking, it'll take forever to get home."

They climbed onto a chunk of granite jutting out of the water and shouted and waved their arms. Ted saw them, pulled up the anchor, and drove over.

"You'd better get in," Ted said. "Lily's looking for you, and she's not happy."

As soon as they jumped on board, Ted steered out of the cove. "You should've seen the bass I almost caught today," he said. "I've been after this one for weeks. Mouth as wide as a trash can. I'm getting close. Sometimes, life is just like fishing: you have to put in the time and pay close attention. Notice the nibbles. And when the time is right, *whammo*—you set the hook."

Cory and Tyra took deep breaths to try to calm down. How much trouble was in store for them?

"What were you doing out in the woods?" Ted asked over the roar of the motor.

"Just some exploring," Tyra answered.

"Find anything interesting?" Ted asked.

Tyra wanted to tell someone about the cabin they'd found, but this seemed like a secret they should keep. "Nothing but a lot of rocks and trees."

Ted gave them a long, assessing look, which made Tyra notice every smear of mud and all the scratches and scrapes on her and Cory. "Is that so?" said Ted. "Nothing else?"

"Nope," said Tyra.

"We got lost," Cory added.

They turned around a rocky point and saw Cory's boat tied up across the cove. Tyra thought maybe she could sneak through the woods back to the barn after all. But as they neared the shore, two figures walked out from under the trees: Rudy and Lily.

Tyra and Cory jumped out of Ted's boat into the shallow water and waded onto dry land but were afraid to get too close to their grandparents. It was hard to tell who was angrier, because they were so deathly quiet. It didn't take much of a glance from Lily for Ted to get the hint. He waved a solemn farewell to Tyra and Cory, and, with a jingle of his hooks, roared off down the lake.

Lily spoke first. "According to Rudy, back home in Boston, Tyra is a well-behaved child. I've known her father since he was a boy, and I believe he would've raised her to know better than to run off. This leads me to the embarrassing conclusion that my own grandson has become a bad influence on other children. I hardly know what to say to you, Cory. Get in the boat. Once we get home, I will find a way to make my displeasure clear."

Cory followed behind his grandmother, head hung low, as they walked along the path, out of sight.

Once they'd gone, Grandpa Rudy and Tyra walked through the woods to Rudy's cabin. She kept waiting for him to say something, but his silence was harsher than words.

Back inside the kitchen, he pointed for her to sit on one of the chairs.

"Were you and Cory digging at the site this morning?"

"No. We'd never try to steal your treasure. It was an accident. We were just looking for a place for a picnic. He came by, and I was so sick of scraping—"

"No digging?"

"No. Honest."

Grandpa Rudy's wrinkles deepened, not with anger, but with worry. "Someone was digging there this morning, and it wasn't me. I've been noticing things all summer, ever since you arrived. Even for the past few summers, I've had a sense that someone has been watching, keeping an eye on my progress. People have died for this treasure. It isn't safe for you to sneak around in the woods. Understand?"

Tyra swallowed hard. Could someone really be stalking them? Someone scarier than Grandpa Rudy?

"You won't see Cory for a few days. I guarantee that Lily will have him working until he can't stand."

"But—"

"No argument."

#

They didn't speak another word all through dinner, or even as Tyra got ready for bed. But that night, before he left to go digging, Grandpa Rudy stopped by Tyra's door.

"I'm going to lock the back door," he said. "Don't go out and don't let anyone inside."

He left without screwing the door shut. Tyra watched him walk into the dark, but she didn't get out of bed. She scanned all around the barn, looking for a shadowy figure following her grandfather. Would he be safe out there?

She lay in bed listening to the wind in the trees. Was that the sound of someone opening the door. Should she tell Grandpa Rudy about the cabin? Could he ever trust her? Who else was out there?

Chapter Eleven

A black fly bit behind Tyra's ear, and she tried to rub it away with the back of her hand. The rest of her hand was covered in red paint. Dressed in a pair of Grandpa Rudy's old overalls, with the legs cut off at the knees, Tyra returned to painting. Together, she and Grandpa Rudy had covered half the barn. As with the scraping, he worked up on the ladder, and she painted from the ground to as high as she could reach.

They'd been out here forever, and Tyra was pretty sure her arms were going to fall off any second. How would Grandpa Rudy explain to her parents why their daughter had no arms?

The sound of exaggerated throat clearing turned Tyra and Rudy's heads toward the path from the dock, where they saw Lily and a sheepish-looking Cory. Lily nudged him with her elbow, and he stepped forward.

"Mr. Palmer, I apologize for talking Tyra into leaving her chores and getting lost in the woods. I won't be a bad influence anymore. Tyra, I'm sorry I got you into trouble." Once he finished, he stubbed his toes in the dirt, again and again.

"Apology accepted," Grandpa Rudy said, as he climbed down from the ladder.

"Do you have a spare paintbrush?" Lily asked.

"I'm sure I could find one."

Tyra noticed that Cory was wearing old, ragged clothes. Did Grandpa Rudy and Lily discuss this on the phone ahead of time?

Soon, Cory was painting side by side with Tyra, while Rudy and Lily watched approvingly.

"Tyra, I know you've been working hard these past few days. And you can believe that Cory has, too. So I'd like to invite you and Rudy to dinner again tonight, and we'll all start fresh, okay?" Lily offered.

Tyra smiled, relieved to have someone be nice to her again. Couldn't Lily give Grandpa Rudy some lessons on what it was like to be a proper grandparent? "Thank you."

"We'll, uh, see what we can do," said Grandpa Rudy.

"I mean a fresh start for *all* of us," Lily said firmly.

Grandpa Rudy looked at Lily and swallowed hard. "Tyra might not be ready tonight, not after all this."

Lily took him by the arm and pulled him away from the kids, but not far enough to keep them from hearing.

"I don't want to tell you how to live your life, Rudy, but I'd better not hear any more about that girl's door being nailed shut every night. You're a better man than that. She's a good girl, and you know it. She's just got a stubborn streak, like her grandfather."

Tyra didn't dare turn around, but she imagined that Grandpa Rudy was as red as the paint all over her hands. "Lily, someone else has been out there, looking, digging."

"You need to pull your head out of those holes and pay attention to what's in front of you. Before it's too late."

Lily left him standing there, twisting his hands together. She walked past Tyra and Cory on her way back to the dock. "You all keep working up an appetite. Ted was out fishing last night and caught a whole mess of bullheads."

#

Tyra and Cory cleaned up after painting and drove Grandpa Rudy's boat to the lodge for dinner. This time, Rudy gave Tyra a whole armful of flowers, black-eyed Susans, for Lily. "Tell her these flowers make me think of her." He'd gone back to the barn, looking miserable.

Tyra wished he'd come to dinner, just once. Maybe if he did, he'd feel less sour. Was he going to spend the night looking at those old photo albums again? Would anything ever let him push past the memory of Grandma Betty?

As they tied up at the lodge's dock, Tyra gathered up the flowers. "Have they always been like this?" she asked Cory.

"Who?"

"Your grandmother and my grandfather?"

"Like what?"

Tyra shook her head sadly. Boys were so clueless. Flowers were clearly a lot more important than raspberries. Anyone could see that.

Before heading to the dining room, Tyra logged into the computer. There were eight more messages from Adriana and Déjà.

Subject: Moose?

You saw a moose? A live one? No way! We looked it up on Wikipedia, and they're freaky. I would've screamed so hard, I would've woken up the whole lake.

We didn't see no mooses, meeses, whatever, but we did see a big rat coming out of the old Kittredge Mansion. Déjà thinks there must be a thousand of them in there.

Did you catch a fish and actually touch it? Ick!

Don't let mean people get you down. You just let us know who they are, and we'll come beat them up for you. Gotta be tough, girl.

4ever urs, Adriana

Subject: WHERE ARE YOU?????

Tyra,

You stopped writing. Do they have you locked up?! Should we call the police? Use the knife to dig your way out. Did your plan fail in a really really bad way? You've got us scared.

But we can't pick you up. My mom's car got smashed last night, when some crackhead crashed into it when he was being chased by the cops. He's lucky the cops got to him before my mom did, she was so mad!

Search party? Email us.

Xxxx oooooo
From ur worried sistah, Déjà

Subject: Here I am

Hi Adriana and Déjà!

My plan did fail in a bad way, and I got in big trouble. I will never, ever complain about doing chores at my house again. I had to scrape the paint off a whole barn!!!

Then I escaped and got in even BIGGER trouble. But me and Cory found a secret cabin in the woods. Grandpa Rudy is worried someone is trying to steal his treasure. What if he's right? Tonight I get to go to the lodge and eat with people who don't spend all their time digging holes.

I'm going to look at more of Grandpa's books and see what was in that buried safe. Was it really gold? What would someone do to get it?

Watch out for those rats.

Love, Tyra

#

Lily was speechless at the sight of the flowers. Tyra had never seen her speechless before. "These are more than just his way of saying sorry for not being here," Tyra said.

"What am I going to do about that man?" Lily said as she placed them in a big vase and put it where she could admire the bouquet through dinner.

The tables were full of food and guests, with a happy summer hum in the air. Cory leaned over to Tyra. "See how clean those windows are? She made me wash all the windows in the entire lodge and in every cabin. Twice."

Walter reached his big hairy arm across the table and dished himself a filet of steaming fried fish. "I guess you do actually catch a fish once in a while, Ted. Nice work."

Ted smiled broadly as he watched his fellow guests dig into the results of his labors. "I was out most of last night, hauling them in. Too bad Rudy didn't come to dinner, so I could show him. He doesn't believe I ever catch anything."

Walter turned toward Tyra. "How is your grandfather? Does he really go out at night to dig for buried treasure?"

Tyra studied Walter and his bushy beard and eyebrows. Why was he interested? Suddenly, Tyra felt protective of her grandfather and his secret activity. Walter was the one telling all those stories about Emerald Eddie—did he know more than he was letting on? And then there was Ted and his round, red face and sweaty smile. Sure, he'd rescued her and Cory from a long walk around the lake, but he could be spying on her grandfather with those binoculars. Why was he always lurking around? Was Meredith, with her lacy turquoise shawl, merely a nice middle-aged lady, or was that a disguise? She kept smiling at her and Cory with her syrupy smile. Even the honeymooners, Tim and Becky, seemed less innocent now. Maybe their whole cuddly thing was just an act to make them appear harmless.

So she lied a small lie: "I have no idea. I'm asleep at night, so I wouldn't know."

Cory, who was unaware of her promise, said, "You told me he goes out every night."

Tyra shot Cory a hard look, and he realized he'd said too much and changed the subject. "You should see some of the stuff we found in the woods, in this old abandoned cabin. I found a cool bottle, and Tyra found a mirror off an old car."

"Back in New Orleans, I collect and sell antiques," Meredith said in her gentle drawl. "Ours is a city with incredible history, though so much was lost in the hurricane and flood. You should let me see your bottle, Cory. It might be worth something."

At the thought that perhaps he had found something valuable, Cory leaped from the table and fetched their lunch bag from the other day. He took out the bottle and handed it to Meredith.

She examined it, holding it up to the light. Tyra looked at Meredith's hands and noticed a tiny bit of earth ground into the knuckle of her pinkie. From digging, perhaps? "This is a soda bottle from the late nineteen twenties. It's unusual to find one completely intact. There's not even a chip on it."

"Is it worth anything?" Cory asked.

"Maybe fifty dollars," Meredith said, as she handed back the bottle. "I would be interested in it for my store. Or anything else you find. The rich history of Spirit Lake makes it even more valuable."

Cory cradled his prize, his eyes aglow at the thought that he'd found such valuable treasure.

"We might look for more tomorrow," he suggested to Tyra.

"What about the mirror?" Tyra asked Meredith.

"I am afraid I know nothing about automobiles," said Meredith.

Walter leaned forward, intensely interested. "I restore old cars for a living. Let's see what you've got." Tyra handed him the mirror.

He turned it over and over in his hands. "Oh, no way! You've got to be kidding. It can't be. Where did you get this?"

"We told you. Out in the woods."

"This isn't just any old mirror," Walter said. "I'd swear it's . . . It couldn't be."

"Walter, what sort of story are you cooking up?" Lily demanded.

Walter got up from the table and walked over to the framed photograph on the wall that showed Emerald Eddie, his son, and the fantastic car. He held the mirror up next to the photo so they could all see it. Its curve and shape matched the one on the car exactly.

"Emerald Eddie's Cadillac," Walter announced. There was a collective intake of breath from around the table.

"Are you serious?" Ted asked.

"I might be able to do something with that in my shop after all," Meredith volunteered.

Walter handed the mirror back to Tyra. "If you find the rest of that car, come see me right away. A man could wait a lifetime to get his hands on a car like that."

For the first time Tyra could remember, Honeymooner Tim spoke something other than a sweet nothing to Becky, though when he spoke, his eyes never left the face of his pretty young bride. "Where did you say you found that stuff again?"

Tyra gave Cory a hard look. "We were lost in the woods," she said. "It was just out there somewhere."

Tyra held the mirror in her lap for the rest of dinner, as the atmosphere in the dining room crackled around her. What if Emerald Eddie's treasure was real? Now, thanks to the mirror, everyone was thinking it was. Would Grandpa Rudy be upset that she didn't tell him about the mirror and the cabin? If she told him now, he'd be furious with her.

#

After dinner, as Cory walked with Tyra through the lodge, gentle footsteps shuffled up behind them. Meredith.

"Pardon me for intruding. Please, wait up, you two," she called. They stopped, and she smiled down at them warmly. Maybe a little too warmly, Tyra thought. "It's lovely to see two children with such freedom on their hands. Brings back the days of my youth on the bayou. My brother used to lead me on grand adventures, under the Spanish moss and around the alligators and water moccasins."

"Gators," Cory said. "I sure wish we had them up here."

"Oh, no. Bayou gators are foul tempered, best avoided at all costs."

Tyra had a hard time picturing Meredith, with her flowing clothes and jangling bracelets, dodging hungry alligators.

"I was wondering two things," Meredith continued. "First, whether either of you might part with your newfound treasures. For the bottle, I could give you thirty dollars now, or take it on consignment. As for the mirror, perhaps you could let me bring it to auction. It could fetch hundreds of dollars, if its origin can be authenticated."

Tyra felt the weight of the mirror in the bag and considered whether she'd be willing to trade it away for a few hundred dollars. Now that she knew it was Emerald Eddie's, it had a story behind it. It wasn't some random broken car part—it was connected to gangsters and ghosts.

"In addition, I want to ask if you would be willing to transport me to the site of your discovery. I could discern whether there are any additional items of value. I would pay you to bring me there, of course. Twenty dollars. Did I say twenty? I meant twenty-five dollars—each —to bring me there. And I would offer a finder's fee for any items we recover."

Despite her Southern charm, Meredith had a hungry gleam in her eyes. Maybe she'd learned a few tricks from those gators and water moccasins after all.

"Let us think about it, okay?" Tyra said, before Cory could accept the offer.

"That is perfectly understandable. You should be cautious, of course. But I promise you will do better with a professional guiding you. Think it over. Y'all have a lovely evening."

Meredith turned and swished off to her cabin, leaving Tyra and Cory alone with the moose head and the stuffed bear.

"Are you crazy?" Cory said. "That's real money."

"We were lost. We don't even know where it was."

"We could look. And we'd better start, before someone else finds it."

"I don't trust her. Let's think it over, okay? And don't go searching without me."

"I won't. I promise."

Tyra knew Cory would keep his promise as long as he could. But the lure of treasure was drawing all sorts of things out of people these days. Maybe Grandpa Rudy wasn't crazy to be so paranoid.

Chapter Twelve

The next morning, Rudy informed Tyra that they needed to go into town for more supplies. "I forgot that two people eat so much more than one."

"I can stay here." If there was one place Tyra did not want to go with Rudy, it was to that store with those stupid old men and their stares.

"No. I intend to keep an eye on you, young lady." His tone made it clear that this was not open to negotiation.

Tyra thought about pretending to feel sick, or falling down and twisting her ankle, or bumping her head, so she wouldn't have to go. But if she did go to town, she could ask to visit with Cory, even if it meant helping with his chores while Grandpa Rudy shopped. Then she wouldn't have to go inside the store, and she and Cory could dream up a scheme to find the cabin again.

As they approached the marina, it became clear that Tyra's plan was doomed. Cory was driving one of the lodge's fishing boats, loaded with guests, who were heading out on a guided fishing trip. The boat lay low in the water, with four extra people on board, all decked out with bright-orange life jackets, tourist caps, and sunglasses. Cory waved as they drew closer.

"When will you be back?" Tyra called.

"Not until late. But maybe we can go frog hunting at Miller's Swamp tomorrow."

Then he was gone, and Tyra was stuck with Grandpa Rudy and shopping.

As they neared the store, Lily was on her way out the door, carrying a bag of supplies. She shook her finger at Rudy. "We missed you again last night, Rudy. I'm starting to think that either you don't like me or you don't like my cooking."

"Now, Lily," Rudy grumbled, his neck growing pink.

"I guess after all these years I should finally get the message. Your granddaughter, at least, has excellent manners. She's a delight to have at the table. And full of surprises."

"Did she give you the flowers?"

"Yes, she did."

"Um, good. Did you like them?"

"Next time, deliver them in person or don't send anything at all."

She walked away, without even waiting for Grandpa Rudy to stop stammering. It all happened so fast that Tyra didn't have a chance to volunteer to help in Lily's kitchen.

Inside the store, the same old men were gathered around the same table, drinking coffee, just like before. And once again, as soon as Tyra walked in the door, they fell silent and stared at her. But this time, the silence lasted for only a moment. A thin man with droopy ears called out, "Well, look who's integrating Spirit Lake."

Someone turned to the man and explained, "Oh, you missed it. This is the little black girl that Dave adopted."

Rudy planted himself squarely in front of the men. "This is Tyra, my granddaughter. And you lunkheads better stop talking like she isn't standing right next to me. If any of you have a problem with her or her skin color, keep your mouth shut about it or else meet me outside."

The men froze and shut their mouths. None of them volunteered to meet Grandpa Rudy outside. One man with a large, round pockmarked nose stuttered an apology. "We . . . we didn't mean any harm, Rudy. We were just—"

Grandpa Rudy cut him off with a look. The men nervously sipped their coffee, while the balding clerk at the counter pretended to study a stack of receipts. Grandpa Rudy put a strong, protective hand on Tyra's shoulder as they walked through the store and filled their basket, and she felt a new warmth spreading inside her.

#

When they got home, Grandpa Rudy put away the groceries. The silence from the store had stayed with them on the boat, and even back inside. But now, for the first time, Tyra knew Grandpa Rudy was willing to claim her as his granddaughter. She used to think she didn't matter to him and that she could be okay with that. She'd been certain that her parents and Grandma Feather were enough family for her. But she'd been wrong. Grandfathers mattered, too. This grandfather mattered.

She went into her room and came back carrying the mirror she'd found in the cabin. She set it down on the counter in front of Grandpa Rudy, an offering.

He stared at it in stunned surprise. "Where did you get that?"

"In the woods, with Cory. We found an old cabin when we were running away from you."

Without even touching the mirror, Grandpa Rudy walked across the room to a case with shelves and a series of drawers. He pulled out a key and unlocked one of the drawers. Inside was a mirror that matched the one Tyra had found. She just about fell over.

"I found this when I was wandering around the woods after Betty died. I've been searching for the rest of the car ever since. It's from a nineteen twenty-eight Cadillac 341A Town Sedan. Emerald Eddie's car. Show me where you found that mirror."

Chapter Thirteen

Tyra sat in the front of the boat, studying the shoreline. When they'd started searching, Grandpa Rudy was as happy as she'd ever seen him. He'd been digging for that treasure for years, but it had been a long time since he'd had a glimmer of hope of finding it.

He had not been thrilled to hear that she'd shown the mirror to the entire lodge, but at least she and Cory had had the sense to keep mum about where they'd found it. Grandpa Rudy was certain they could find the cabin and treasure first, if they moved fast. But what would he do if he found it? He didn't care much about money or buying things. Would he be a different person if the search wasn't part of his life anymore? What would that new person be like? Tyra hoped it would make him happy.

Now they'd been out for a couple of hours, up and down the lake, and Tyra still had no idea where they should land. From the water, the shore appeared completely different than it did from the woods. It was one solid wall of trees, punctuated here and there by chunky gray rocks. She wasn't even sure which cove they should explore. When she and Cory had hiked home, they were mostly trying to avoid tripping and falling into the lake and drowning (and meeting the ghost of Emerald Eddie). And then they got a ride from Ted. Now she saw an island out in the water that looked familiar, but when they drove closer, she spied three other islands scattered around the lake. Which island was the right one? Her memories blurred together.

Grandpa Rudy asked the same question he'd been asking for hours: "Where did you come out?" Each time he asked, the frustration in his voice rose a notch. And Tyra's irritation matched his.

"I don't know. We were just trying to get home."

"There must've been a rock or some sort of landmark. Something."

"I don't know. We were lost."

"Think!"

But no matter how hard she thought, nothing jumped out at her, and the more they looked, the fuzzier her memories became.

#

They went ashore three times before giving up. Each time, they wandered around the woods, but Tyra knew they weren't in the right place. There was no clearing, no cabin. They were not going to find it from the water.

#

They tried a different tactic. They drove the boat back home and then hiked into the woods to the dig site where he'd stumbled upon Tyra and Cory.

"I was coming up this path," he said. "Where were the two of you?"

"Over here," Tyra said, climbing onto the picnic rock. "We were eating lunch. When we heard you, we ducked behind this rock. We couldn't get past you, so we ran into the woods."

"Let's see if we can figure out which way you went."

Tyra closed her eyes and imagined that afternoon, how it felt to see her grandfather sneaking up the path with that pick handle raised up high, how terrified she and Cory had been. She imagined them counting: *one, two, three.* When she opened her eyes, she knew where to go.

She led them through the woods, but when she reached the first fork in the path, she couldn't remember which way to go. She backed up and approached the fork again, trying to recall the moment. It didn't work; she was moving too slowly. She and Cory had been running, so she went back and ran down the path. At that speed, as she played back the memory of hearing the shouts behind them, she naturally took the left-hand fork. Grandpa Rudy jogged along behind her, struggling to keep up.

"Wait. Slow down," he called. "I'm not as young as you."

Tyra stopped, and this time when she looked back, instead of seeing an angry ogre, she just saw her grandfather—an old man, out of breath.

They traveled along the path to the giant tree with the vines. She turned to Grandpa Rudy excitedly. "We stopped here. We thought we'd lost you, but you were still behind us."

"I didn't get much farther than this. But I didn't know it was you. I thought it was whoever had been digging at the site, maybe someone dangerous, someone who might've hurt you and Cory. When you weren't at the house, I hoped you two had just gone fishing."

Knowing her grandfather had been worried about her helped take away some of the sting from the angry shouting she'd heard that day, and all that followed.

She led them deeper into the woods, along a narrow trail that her grandfather said was a deer path, up a hill, then down the loose, rocky slope she and Cory had slid down. She waited at the bottom for Grandpa Rudy to pick his way through the rocks—even though he was tough as a wolverine, he was too old to hurl himself down slippery hills.

At the edge of the bog, Tyra stopped. The light was different this time, dimmer, and she realized that the sun was starting to set behind the mountains.

"I don't remember where we went next."

"You've been doing great so far. Trust your instincts. Are we close?"

"There was an old road, all overgrown. We followed it to the cabin. Though you could hardly see the cabin from there. You could walk right past it."

"So all we have to do is find the road. Let's walk around this swamp, and maybe we'll see it."

"But I don't know which way."

"Just try."

Tyra was tired and hungry. Mosquitoes from the bog whined in her ears, hovered around her head, and feasted on the backs of her knees. She didn't know which way to go, but she knew she couldn't stand near this swamp for one more second.

Maybe she took the wrong way, because when she hurried into the woods on the other side, still brushing away clouds of biting bugs, she couldn't see the road. Just a bunch of pine trees. The growing darkness didn't help.

She stood between the trees and stopped. "This doesn't look right."

Grandpa Rudy walked in circles, searching for a trace of the old road. Tyra just wanted to lie down and go to sleep. She found a fallen log and sat with her head in her hands.

All day they'd been looking, and now they were as lost as ever. Lost deep in the woods, with night approaching. There was a chill in the air, and she was only wearing shorts and a T-shirt. She shivered, and her breath came out with a little quaver, like she might cry. She didn't want to cry; she never liked crying. And she especially didn't want to cry in front of Grandpa Rudy. But she didn't want to spend all night in the woods, in the dark with the mosquitoes and animals.

Grandpa Rudy walked over to her. "Hey, come on. Help me look."

"I want to go home."

"Just a little longer. We've got to be close."

"I'm tired and hungry and cold. It's getting dark. Do you even know where we are?"

"Not exactly. I didn't think Emerald Eddie had come this far east. I've never been in this section of the woods before."

"We're lost! We're going to be stuck here all night!"

"Don't worry. I'll get us home," Grandpa Rudy reassured her. He pulled a small yellow gadget out of his backpack and turned it on.

"What's that?"

"A GPS. It uses satellites to tell us exactly where we are. It can help point the way home."

Her grandfather owned an electronic device? "You don't even use a computer. You don't have a TV. How can you have a GPS?"

He shrugged. "I spend a lot of time in the woods. I make maps. It's the tool I need. I may be old, but I'm not an idiot." He waved the device around in front of his body. "I'm having trouble picking up the satellites. Let's try over here."

He stepped through the woods, holding the device in the air, trying to get a reading. As they walked, Tyra calmed down a little. If this thing worked, maybe they would get home tonight after all.

Then she saw the big oak trees, near the edge of the bog. That's where the road passed by. If she didn't say anything and

Grandpa Rudy got his GPS thingy to work, they could go home and eat dinner, and she could spend the night sleeping in an actual bed. They could come back another day. Or she might never find this place again. Her brain was racing: should she speak up, or should she keep her mouth shut?

"I know where we are now," she said.

"What?"

"The road goes past those big trees over there." She pushed through the underbrush, making her way to the oaks. Just beyond was the road, barely visible in the gloom.

"Where is this road on my old maps? Was this a secret path?" Grandpa Rudy said, mostly to himself.

They walked together down the overgrown road, along the crumbling old stone wall, until they found the clearing with the pines on one side and the huge boulder and rock pile on the other. In the growing darkness, it looked like an old abandoned parking area or campground.

"Where is it?" Grandpa Rudy asked.

With a smile, Tyra walked to the edge of the clearing and pushed back the brush and fallen branches to reveal the hidden cabin.

Chapter Fourteen

Grandpa Rudy was too excited to speak. He dug in his backpack for a flashlight and twisted it on. Inside the old cabin, he shook with eagerness, making the light flicker and dance around the crumbling walls. Tyra felt like she did at Christmas when she gave her mom something perfect. Only ten times as much.

"This could be it. This could be his secret cabin. Show me where you found the mirror." His eyes were wide open, as if he was taking in every speck of light, every image.

Tyra led him to a corner full of old branches and leaves. "Maybe a raccoon brought it here," she said. "Don't they like shiny objects?"

"Yes, yes. It could be that. But how far would it have come? I found the other mirror a long way from here, closer to the house, near where Eddie's other cabin was before it burned down. I've been digging there for years—and nothing. Maybe Emerald Eddie and his men buried the safe here. It could be under us right this very second."

Tyra felt a thrill of possibility, but even that wasn't enough to keep her from yawning a great yawn worthy of a lion.

"I should have brought tools," Grandpa Rudy said as he searched every inch of the cabin for another clue. Tyra sat on a set of rusty bed springs, so tired she couldn't stand on her feet for another second. At the sound of the creaking metal, Grandpa Rudy looked over at her, his face hardly visible in the dim light, but his eyes still shining.

"I'm sorry, Tyra. I know you need to go home. I can't do anything more here right now. Let me mark this spot, and we'll leave." He pulled out his GPS again and pushed a button.

"That tells you where we are?" she asked.

"And it'll get us from here to home and help us find this cabin again tomorrow." He chewed on his lip thoughtfully and said, "Thank you, Tyra. For finding this place."

\#

After a dinner of hastily cooked spaghetti and meatballs, they cleared off the dining room table, and Grandpa Rudy spread out his maps and charts. With the GPS, he calculated the distance between home and the old cabin. Soon he was able to pinpoint the exact location on the biggest map. From the pile, he pulled out another map that was crinkled and yellowed with age.

Revived by the food, Tyra admired the old hand-drawn map. It was like the table of contents to a book with a hundred different stories. If they found Emerald Eddie's treasure, they'd be part of one of those chapters. She traced her fingers around the shoreline, to where the newly discovered cabin was hiding.

"This map is from the nineteen twenties," Grandpa Rudy explained. "The path we saw tonight isn't on here. It's not on my other maps, either. Somebody didn't want it to be found. Now it's totally grown over and invisible from the main road. Before I retired, I was a land surveyor in the summers, and I drove a snowplow in the winter. I know the roads and land around here better than anyone. I never saw that path."

"But we know it's there," said Tyra, feeling a lot better now that she had a full belly and an ice-cold glass of soda in front of her. Grandpa Rudy had promised that tomorrow they'd buy ice cream to celebrate. If the treasure was really there, maybe they could have ice cream and soda every day.

"That's right. See all these marks—each X is a place where I've dug. Right here is where I found my mirror. I've searched the woods and hollows for a mile in all directions from that point. I even bought a mask and snorkel to explore underwater along the shore. But the cabin you and Cory found is all the way over here." He took a pencil, and drew a tight, dark circle. "This is the break I've needed." He turned serious again. "No one outside the family can know about these maps, or that we found the cabin. Not even your little friend."

"Cory would never say anything."

"This is a dangerous business. You're a smart kid and a good worker. We can find this together. But you have to swear not to tell."

Tyra swallowed hard. She wanted to be part of this search, but this was a different kind of promise than she'd made before. If she made it, she'd have to keep it. "I swear."

"Good. We'll start digging tomorrow night. It's a shame you showed the mirror to everyone, and even worse that Walter knew what it was. We'll have to work fast. Who knows, maybe we'll even find my uncle Danny."

"Who?"

"He would be your great-great-uncle. He was my father's brother, an expert mechanic and an amateur race car driver—and, from what I've heard, always in trouble. He lived in New York City and Boston, and then he met Emerald Eddie and became his chauffeur. Lucky Danny, they called him. He once won a huge poker game with a royal flush, and after that he always carried an ace of spades in his jacket pocket.

"When I was a kid, I wanted to believe it. Smuggling, guns, treasure. I loved that our family was part of such an exciting story."

"What happened to him?"

"Legend has it that he was driving Emerald Eddie's car when everything went haywire. The police were about to catch them, so they buried a safe full of money, gold, and gems. No one ever saw him again after that. Some say Danny was shot in the woods after they buried the safe. Some say he escaped to Canada."

Grandpa Rudy waved at his carefully ordered bookshelves and filing cabinets. "I've read every book and newspaper article ever written about Emerald Eddie, trying to figure out what happened. A few of them mention Lucky Danny, but none say what happened to him."

"Maybe we'll find a clue tomorrow night," Tyra said.

"We'd better hurry," said her grandfather. "I bet the store sold a bunch of shovels today."

Chapter Fifteen

"Pretend you're in super-slow-motion replay mode," Cory whispered from behind her. Tyra moved the long-handled net slower than she would have thought possible, almost like it wasn't moving at all. She crouched on the end of a log that jutted into the swamp and guided the net toward a bright-green frog with bulging eyes, who squatted placidly on a lily pad.

"Closer . . . closer," Cory coached. "When you swoop in, go as fast as you can. Ready . . . now!"

Tyra smashed the net over the lily pad just as the frog jumped away. He flew into the net, but the thrust threw her off-balance. Teetering, she slipped face-first into the mucky water.

Cory hooted with laughter as Tyra sputtered and spit out mud and weeds, all the while holding the net up high, with the frog trying to squirm his way out. "I got one! I finally got one!" she screamed.

They'd been in the swamp all morning catching frogs. Or at least Cory had been catching them. Tyra had been trying and failing. Now she sloshed her way back onto dry land, and they walked over to a five-gallon bucket in the shade of a willow tree. She pulled off the lid and dumped her frog into the water with the half dozen Cory had already caught.

"Go play with your friends," she said to the frog.

"Nice catch," Cory said. "Now you're an official member of the Frog Hunters Club."

"What should we do with them?" Tyra asked.

"We could take them home and see if Grandma wants to cook them for dinner. I think they eat frogs in France."

Tyra wondered if her parents were eating frogs on their trip. She'd talked to them this morning, before heading out with Cory. Even though she was bursting to tell them about the cabin and the search for Emerald Eddie's loot, she'd pretended that everything was normal. They'd assured her that they were working hard and promised that she was having more fun than they were. Knowing her parents, it was probably true. But they sounded happy. What would they have said if she'd told them she planned to stay up all night digging for buried treasure?

"I don't want to eat the frogs," Tyra said.

"We could use them for bait. Sometimes the super-big bass or pike will go for a frog."

The thought of shoving a hook through the back of a frog made Tyra queasy. "Couldn't we just let them go?"

So they did, and then they drove the boat out of the swamp to a sandy beach not far away. Tyra washed off all the muck, and they dug for freshwater clams and swam and skipped rocks.

As they lay drying in the sun, Cory asked, "Should we try to find that cabin again? Fifty dollars for a dumb old bottle. A little less if we take Meredith's offer now, but still, it'd be money in our pockets. I'm going to buy a fly rod. Fly fishing is for serious fishermen—it's all about technique. Let's go find the cabin."

Tyra really wanted to tell Cory that she and Grandpa Rudy had found it and had made plans for that night, because Cory was her friend and had shown her a million cool things about Spirit Lake. But she had to keep her promise. Whatever happened, she needed to keep Cory from returning. Grandpa Rudy was being nice to her now, but he'd never forgive her if she brought other people back there. Until this summer, she'd never felt like she had a grandfather, even though she knew he was out there. There were a lot of people missing from her life whom she'd probably never meet—not just her birth parents, but all their extended families: birth cousins and aunts and uncles. That was a tiny part of what came with being adopted, and she usually didn't think about it. Having Grandpa Rudy be part of her life was important.

"Nah, I don't want to leave the water. We can find the cabin another day. Let's see who can hold their breath the longest."

She jumped into the lake, and Cory followed behind her.

#

Swimming didn't last long as a diversion, so the next time Cory asked to go to the cabin, Tyra suggested fishing instead. "Shouldn't we be trying to catch some shiners or a whitefish?" she asked. There were only four fish left on his list of fifteen species: golden shiners, whitefish, fallfish, and rainbow smelt.

Cory stared at the water, as though he'd been confronted with a difficult homework problem. "I'll probably need to trap the shiners with a minnow trap, but I'd rather hook one. So far, I haven't had any luck. Some people say you can catch them where you find sunfish. I've been thinking about asking Paul, at the bait shop. He would know."

"Then we'd better go talk to him. Are you serious about catching these fish or not?"

"Sure, I just figured . . . No, you're right. I mean, you want to catch them, too?"

Tyra felt like she was the rope in the middle of a tug-of-war. Cory was her friend, the one person making this summer bearable, but finding this treasure meant more to Grandpa Rudy than to anybody in the world. She needed to keep Cory away from the secret cabin.

"Of course I do. And if you don't stay focused, you might miss out. Especially on the rare fish."

"Shiners aren't exactly rare."

"You don't have one yet."

Cory couldn't argue with her there. They picked up the gear they'd scattered around the beach. As Tyra grabbed her towel, a Spirit Lake Lodge sailboat scooted around the corner of the point. The breeze fluffed the sails of the small craft as it glided steadily toward them. As the sail shifted in the wind, Tyra saw the pilot: Walter.

He was so hairy that he looked like a beast dressed in swim trunks and a T-shirt. Even though he was a big man, he sat perfectly at ease on the sailboat, skillfully adjusting the sails to slide the craft onto the beach, practically at their feet.

"Ahoy there, kids," he said, accompanied by his booming laugh. He quickly dropped the sail, but stayed seated on the gunwale, bobbing on the light waves rolling into the beach.

"Hi Walter," Cory said. "What's up?"

"Lily told me you two were out and about today. I saw you sunning on the beach and was wondering . . . if you're not too busy, maybe you could show me that cabin you found."

Walter suddenly seemed more like Blackbeard the Pirate than a bear. As he smiled, Tyra could imagine a gold tooth glinting in the sun. If she'd learned one thing from her adventure books, it was that, no matter how much pirates smile at you, they can't be trusted.

"We were actually heading back to town," Tyra said quickly, before Cory could volunteer to help.

"I don't want to horn in on your treasure hunting. It's your discovery, okay?" Walter said, almost pleading. "But the Cadillac nineteen twenty-eight 341A Town Sedan, it's just... You can't imagine how beautiful that car was. It's a restorer's dream. No one ever found Emerald Eddie's car. But if you found the mirror..."

"Well, maybe—" Cory began.

"Maybe we could help you look next week," Tyra jumped in. "Come on, Cory." She tossed the picnic basket into the motorboat and jumped on. Cory followed her, a little confused.

"Sorry, Walter," he said. "We can try later, okay?"

Walter hid his disappointment with a smile. "No worries. I guess it's been lost for this long, it can wait a little longer. But in the right hands, that car is worth as much as whatever was in Emerald Eddie's safe. Al Capone's armored 341A sold at auction for more than six hundred thousand dollars. Who knows what condition this car is in, but I can promise a percentage of the final price. Whatever you think is fair—five percent? Plus a couple hundred bucks up front?"

Tyra could see Cory working out the math in his head. It would make for a lot of bait and fishing rods. "Cory, come on. We need to go."

"Oh, right." He pulled the engine to life.

"We'll think it over," Tyra called back to Walter as they drove away.

The smile dropped from Walter's face, and he spoke words of warning: "Don't wait too long."

#

Outside the store, Tyra hesitated. Keeping Cory distracted was important, but going inside the store again, without Grandpa Rudy, seemed impossible. What would the men say or do this time? She hated feeling that hot, unkind spotlight focused on her. She wasn't sure she could do it. Her feet wouldn't move.

Cory waited for her at the screen door. "What's wrong?"
"Nothing."

"What's going on, Tyra? You don't want to stay at the beach, you don't want to talk to Walter, you don't want to search for the cabin again, and now you don't want to go into the store."

"I'm sorry. I'm coming." She willed her feet to move, but it felt like her shoes weighed a hundred pounds.

Cory looked at her with concern. "Are you okay?"
"I'm fine. Let's go."

#

This time, the store was mostly empty. A tourist was at the counter buying sunscreen. The only old man from before was the one with the big pockmarked nose and a spiderweb of veins on his cheeks, but this time, instead of drinking coffee with his pals, he sat behind the bait counter reading a newspaper. This was Paul. He looked up at Cory and Tyra and raised an eyebrow.

"Cory. I heard that you two were pals."

Cory didn't seem to notice the disapproval in Paul's voice, but Tyra did. She wished she'd stayed rooted to the dock outside.

"That's right. Tyra's helping me in my quest."

"For all the fish?" Everyone in Spirit Lake knew about Cory's plan.

"Yup. You should've seen the pike she caught the other day. Thirty-two inches."

Paul's frown was replaced by surprise. "That so? Good for you. I didn't know that bl—that many girls catch pike."

"I did. And frogs, too." Tyra kept her face as tough as she could, trying to channel Grandpa Rudy's glare through her own eyes, to knock Paul off his seat. She wasn't ashamed of being black, and she wasn't going to let Paul make her feel anything but proud of herself.

"And a whole ton of perch and sunnies, smallmouth bass, and two bullheads," Cory boasted of his fishing protégé. "She's a natural."

Paul nodded in acknowledgment, if not actual approval. Tyra didn't care, but she wanted to get out of the store as soon as possible. *This is all to keep the treasure secret and safe,* she reassured herself. She liked to think Grandpa Rudy would be proud of her, too.

Cory continued. "I'm still missing rainbow smelt, fallfish, golden shiners, and whitefish. I was going to shoot for shiners next."

"I can sell you a whole bucket right now," Paul teased.

"You know I have to catch them myself. I've been thinking a trap would count, but it'd be more fun to hook them. Besides, my traps haven't come up with any yet."

"Use corn bread, not white bread, for bait. You can also buy a can of cat food, poke some holes in it, and put it in your trap. Did you try down by Rock Creek?"

Cory nodded.

"Put it closer to the mouth, where the water runs clearer. You could probably hook one, too, but use a small hook—try a number twelve, and only a tiny bit of worm or bread ball."

"Thanks, Paul."

"You'll do it, Cory."

They turned to leave, but Paul called out before they reached the door.

"Little girl. Tyra."

She stopped and braced herself for some painful insult or comment, but she couldn't turn to face him.

"Tell your grandfather to be careful about that treasure. Ghosts aren't the only things lurking in the woods."

#

Subject: Secret message. DO NOT SHARE OR PRINT!

Hi Adriana and Déjà!

I have to write this fast before Cory comes back. I don't want him reading over my shoulder. Tonight me and Grandpa are heading off to find real buried treasure! Seriously!! And we're not the only ones looking. But don't tell anyone. NO ONE. This is SUPER TOP SECRET.

If anything happens to me, I hereby leave my Nintendo games to Adriana. Déjà, you can have my books, including Harry Potter. You should split the stuffed animals.

Have to run.

T.

Chapter Sixteen

Tyra followed her grandfather as they approached the clearing and the cabin. "While you were frog hunting with Cory, I hauled tools and equipment out here. It would've been easier and faster to bring it by boat, but someone might've seen me. Soon I'll be used to the path, and I'll never lose it, not even in the dark."

Inside, he'd set up lights on tripods, powered by car batteries. In the bright glare, the cabin was old and decrepit, not at all like a hiding place for treasure.

Grandpa Rudy explained his theory: "I think Emerald Eddie and his pals drove out here in a desperate hurry, but with enough time to bury the safe. If they buried it in the woods, someone might notice. But if they lifted the floorboards and buried it underneath, no one would see the fresh dirt. What do you think?"

"I guess that could happen." Tyra thought it was a lot of extra work to pull up the floor. Why not just cover the spot with leaves or pine needles?

"Some of the boards don't seem like they were attached tightly in the first place." He pulled the rotten planks away to reveal uneven floor joists and dirt below. "These joists are far apart. All they had to do was move one, and presto! It's probably not even buried very deep, just covered over with a thin layer of dirt."

As dusk gave way to night, they began to take apart the floor of the cabin. Grandpa Rudy gave Tyra an old set of leather work gloves, and as he ripped out the floorboards, Tyra carried them outside to a pile near the cabin. The boards were heavy and awkward, and she had to avoid poking herself on rusty nails. But Tyra was excited to see the growing expanse of bare dirt where the floor had been. She wished there was a big X drawn there, like in the pirate picture books she'd enjoyed as a little kid.

Grandpa started to dig. One shovel at a time, he filled a wheelbarrow parked at the cabin door. Once it was ready, Tyra pushed it over by the pile of floorboards and dumped out the rocks and dirt. Grandpa Rudy used the time between loads to rest, because the lights made it hot inside the cabin. Moths and june bugs hovered in a cloud around the lamps.

They found another old bottle, a broken ceramic plate, and a silver fork, but no treasure. Grandpa Rudy dug and dug, deeper and deeper. They both kept waiting for the sound of steel on steel that would mean he'd found the safe.

#

In the first light of morning, they had to accept that the safe was not buried under the floor of the cabin. Grandpa Rudy threw the old floorboards back inside with a crash. They piled all the dirt that he'd dug back in one corner. Her grandfather looked exhausted, and his beard was full of dust and sweat.

He came back with a final wheelbarrow load. "No one will know we were here," he said. "We should leave before it gets any lighter out."

"I'm sorry it's not the right spot," Tyra said.

"Who says it's not? It's just not buried in the cabin. It was a dumb idea, anyway. Too much trouble to pull up the floor. They must've hidden it somewhere nearby, though. We'll come back tonight and start digging in the yard. I know it's here. It has to be."

Tyra wasn't so sure, but she knew she'd be back that night to dig anyway.

#

After putting away their tools, they ate breakfast and went straight to bed. Spending all night digging holes and moving old lumber can make the brightest, clearest summer day much too bright and much too clear.

Well after noon, Tyra drifted out of sleep long enough to hear her grandfather at the screen door, talking with Cory.

"Is Tyra here?"

"She's sleeping." Tyra wished she could rush out and tell Cory what they'd been up to. Maybe she could convince Grandpa Rudy to let Cory come with them—he was strong and could dig a lot faster that she could. Of course, they'd have to tell Lily, which could be a problem. None of this mattered, though, because Tyra didn't even have the energy to open her eyes all the way.

"Is she sick?"

"Yeah. She'll be back on her feet soon. It's a bug that could last for a few days. I heard on the news that the frog flu is going around. You two weren't catching frogs this week, were you?"

"Yesterday. A whole bunch of them. Down by Miller's Swamp."

"That explains it. You're more used to it, because you catch frogs all the time."

"At least a couple a week."

"That builds resistance. She's from the city, so she's more susceptible. Still, make sure you drink plenty of orange juice and eat lots of vegetables. You don't want to catch it—trust me. Come back in a few days."

Tyra heard the motor on Cory's boat start up and fade away. She fell back to sleep before the sound was gone.

Chapter Seventeen

In the fresh darkness of the night, Grandpa Rudy explained his new theory to Tyra. He paced in front of the cabin, rubbing the backs of his knuckles excitedly.

"They were in a hurry, see? It wasn't a huge safe, but it was heavy. Even though they were all big, burly Irishmen, it was a two-person job to carry it. They would've come barreling down that road, trying not to crash into the trees."

Tyra looked out into the gloom and imagined a huge green car screaming down the dirt road, its tires slipping and spinning. The driver, Uncle Danny, who might have had the same fierce scowl as Grandpa Rudy, gripped the steering wheel tightly, while the other two men kept looking back through the rear window to see if they were being followed. The safe was hidden under picnic supplies and blankets. Emerald Eddie himself had a broad grin on his face because he thrived on danger.

Grandpa Rudy walked to the edge of the circles of light cast by the lanterns. "They sped down here and slammed on the brakes. They needed a plan, fast. Emerald Eddie knew it's not so easy to both hide a safe and leave yourself a way to get it back. If you don't want anyone to ever find it, just take it out in the boat and send it to the bottom of the lake. Spirit Lake was carved by glaciers, and parts are more than a hundred feet deep. But there was a lot of gold and cash in that safe, and he wanted it back. He needed to bury it. Where?"

"In the woods?" Tyra asked, scrunching up her face, trying to think like a gangster.

"But it's rocky. And if you're searching for a safe that was buried yesterday, you just have to find a bunch of fresh dirt."

"You could pile rocks or branches over it."

Grandpa Rudy pointed an approving finger at her. "That's good. Now you're thinking. But what if you bury it in a place where you can't tell whether the dirt's been disturbed? There are lots of weeds here now, but back then this road and cabin were new. This whole parking area would've been bare dirt."

"So they could've buried it right here, in front of the cabin?"

Grandpa Rudy held his hands in front of him as if he were driving a big car down the road. He steered over to the enormous boulder and rock pile that loomed on the edge of the clearing. "They'd park over here by this big rock, leave the car, and dig a hole in the middle of this flat area. Once they'd covered it, no one could tell they were ever here."

Tyra looked down at her feet. She could be standing over the safe with all its golden treasure right this second. The bottoms of her feet tingled. "Where should we start?"

Closing his eyes, Grandpa Rudy stepped from the imaginary car, as if he were carrying a heavy safe. With seven or eight paces, he reached the middle of the grass in front of the cabin. He opened his eyes. "Right here." He scratched an *X* in the ground with the heel of his boot. "Let's start digging."

#

They dug and dug and dug. "We need to go down two feet," Grandpa Rudy told Tyra with confidence. "The safe was no more than two feet high, so they'd need a hole close to three feet deep. That's a big hole to dig in a hurry, but this driveway is sandy, so they could do it. All we need to do is find the top of the safe."

He'd marked off a square of ground fifteen feet on a side. Two feet down was a lot deeper than Tyra had expected, and though the soil was sandy, there were plenty of rocks, which shivered the nerves in her hands each time she struck one with the shovel.

Grandpa Rudy had excavated half of the square, while Tyra poked away in one corner.

"Don't just stand there," Grandpa Rudy barked. "Dig!"

"I need another break."

"You've spent more time on breaks than digging."

That was completely unfair. Tyra had been digging all night long, when she should have been sleeping. Just because her crazy grandfather had searched for this buried safe for thirty years didn't mean it had to be there. It just meant he was crazy, and if she spent all night digging, maybe that made her crazy, too. She glared at her grandfather until he shrugged and went back to his shovel.

The people who had actually used this cabin didn't spend their time digging. They came here to have fun. Tough men and pretty young women, dressed in those funny one-piece bathing suits, like in the old black-and-white movies. When she was little, Tyra's dad convinced her that the reason old movies were in black and white was that color itself hadn't been invented yet. He was always saying goofy stuff like that.

Maybe the people had hung a rope swing down by the water, so they could fly out into the lake. They'd spent the night playing guitars and accordions and singing around the fire, as sparks shot up into the night. They'd told stories about robbing banks and breaking through roadblocks. And they must have roasted marshmallows. There's no point being around a campfire unless you roast marshmallows.

The sound of metal on metal interrupted Tyra's daydreams. Grandpa Rudy looked up with an excited smile.

A flurry of digging revealed . . . the rusty chrome handle to a car door.

Tyra's heart sank down to her dusty sneakers. No safe full of gold.

But Grandpa Rudy examined the piece of metal closely, as if it were a precious ancient relic. "It's from a Cadillac."

"Seriously?"

"I've memorized every square inch of that car. We're getting close." He started digging with new vigor, and Tyra watched the pile of excavated dirt grow taller.

"Why are parts of Emerald Eddie's car scattered all over the place?" she asked.

"Maybe they ditched it in the woods, or he sent Uncle Danny off with the car to lure the cops away. Maybe in the chase they crashed into trees and rocks, so by the time they got here, one of the mirrors was hanging off the side of the car, and the door handle was almost banged all the way off. The mirror and handle fell off when they hid the car nearby."

Grandpa Rudy had a knack for telling a convincing story about why they should dig in a certain spot. This happened, then this, then this . . . so this is where the treasure should be.

That night, they didn't have the story straight. When the entire fifteen-foot square was emptied of two feet of dirt, there was no sign of a safe. With wide-toothed rakes, Grandpa Rudy and Tyra refilled the hole. Afterward, Rudy marked the square on the map. "Tomorrow, we'll dig closer to the cabin," he said, as he folded the map under the lamp. Its light seemed dimmer now, but Tyra realized it was merely the dawn creeping through the woods.

In all these summers spent digging, how many different stories had Grandpa Rudy told himself? Was it just a matter of figuring out the story that would lead to digging in the exact right spot?

Chapter Eighteen

Tyra and Grandpa Rudy stood frozen at the back door to his house. Grandpa Rudy never left without locking up, yet the door was unlocked now. Not open, but unlocked.

"Wait out here," Grandpa Rudy said firmly. He inched open the door, holding a short-handled shovel at the ready. He disappeared inside, and Tyra waited anxiously, listening for a *crash-bang*, the sound of a struggle, or worse. If she did hear something, how would she get help? Should she hop into the boat and drive into town? Find Lily? Tyra took two steps toward the dock, preparing for escape.

Silence. Somewhere in the woods, a squirrel chattered.

She jumped when Grandpa Rudy reappeared. "No one here," he said. "Maybe they heard us coming."

Is this how the three bears felt after Goldilocks broke into their home, Tyra wondered, as she followed Grandpa Rudy inside. Something felt creepy in there now. They walked through the house looking for clues, for a sign that something had been taken.

"This topographic map wasn't on the top of the pile," Grandpa Rudy said, standing by the table. "When we left, the county survey map was on top. Wasn't it?"

Tyra wasn't sure. She was certainly glad none of the maps they'd left behind had the cabin marked on them. Those maps always traveled strapped to Grandpa Rudy's back, in their protective black tube. Paranoia was just another word for caution, if people were really out to steal your treasure.

The file cabinets in the living room were closed, but Tyra noticed that one drawer wasn't shut all the way. "Someone's been in this drawer," she whispered.

He pulled it open. There were so many files, it would be hard for most people to notice if just one or two had been taken. But Grandpa Rudy always put his files away neatly, so he knew that the intruder had read through the drawer quickly and stuffed the papers back into the folders.

"They're getting bold," Grandpa Rudy said. "They must sense that we're close to finding the treasure. We're going to have to be extra careful."

Tyra walked to her bedroom and slumped down on the bed, almost asleep already. Who would have broken into the house? A mysterious stranger, or someone they knew? Walter? Meredith? Paul? So many people might be coveting the treasure. What would they be willing to do to get their hands on it?

#

Tyra picked up her shovel and poked at the shadowy dirt. A patchwork of fifteen-foot squares spread out in front of the cabin, like a giant quilt. Each time, Grandpa Rudy had found a different logic for why the treasure should be buried in that particular spot. Tyra didn't want to hear any more stories.

If they found the treasure, it would make Grandpa Rudy happy in a way that most people never get to be happy. How often does someone spend year after year searching for something and finally find it? But her shoulders hurt, the blisters on her hand were turning into calluses, and her back ached like she was an old lady. She had twenty-three mosquito bites in various stages of itchiness.

And she wanted to be out in the sun, fishing and swimming with Cory. She wanted to laugh. Grandpa Rudy was nicer now, but he wasn't exactly a barrel of fun. Not like Cory, who always had a goofy expression on his face or a crazy plan for a new adventure.

Grandpa Rudy hacked away at the outline of a large circle with the long-handled pick. The potential closeness of the treasure acted like a special battery for him. Tyra didn't have any source of power at the moment. She sighed a long sigh.

"What's the matter?" Grandpa Rudy asked, not pausing from scraping a line in the earth.

She just shook her head.

"Come on, we've barely started. Tonight's the night. See this old charcoal? This is where they had a fire pit. See how this rock is scorched on one side?"

Grandpa Rudy picked up a large round stone that was blackened on one half. "If they hid the safe directly under the fire pit, no one would think to look there. Even their friends wouldn't know, and no one wants to steal your treasure more than your friends."

Tyra thought of Cory and Déjà and Adriana. None of them would steal anything of hers. "You have to be able to trust your friends," she said.

"When it comes to gold, sometimes the people who seem to be your friends really aren't. And anyway, Emerald Eddie was a criminal and probably assumed everyone else was like him."

After so many nights awake, Tyra felt dull and numb, as if she were living underwater. She started shoveling. There were a few charred bits of wood in there, so Grandpa Rudy could be right. But the ground was hard and full of rocks. If Emerald Eddie and his men only had shovels, it would have taken forever to dig a deep hole. Nothing in Grandpa Rudy's story made her shovel any lighter or the night any brighter. A mosquito flew past her ear, and Tyra slapped at it.

"The mosquitoes are killing me," she whined. "I won't have any blood left by morning."

"One big hole tonight. That's all. You understand the reasons why it'll be here, right?"

"You always have a story. But it's always just that—a story."

"Sometimes in life, you have a sense about things. And this time, I've got that sense."

"You're always saying that. Except there's nothing out here but dirt and rocks and trees and mosquitoes."

"Why don't you grab a snack? There are apples, cookies, and sandwiches in the pack. You could have an early drunch." That was the word they'd created for dinner in the dark.

"I don't want to eat my drunch. I don't want to stay awake all night. I don't want to dig holes. I want to play with my friend and swim in the lake and go fishing and see the sun."

"Tyra Palmer, you are not a quitter. In this family, we don't give up. Not ever."

"This is stupid! I don't want to be here!" Tyra screamed, as she hurled her shovel across the clearing, out into the dark.

In the shadows from the lanterns, Grandpa Rudy's face was full of hard lines. His brows met in a deep frown. "Go pick up that shovel. Now."

Tyra glared at him, but his angry gaze matched her own. She snatched one of the lanterns and marched across the clearing to find the shovel.

There probably weren't any stupid gangsters. Emerald Eddie was probably just a story that someone made up, and Grandpa Rudy believed it because he needed something to do after Grandma Betty died, and he was mean and had no friends, so this kept him busy. But Tyra had better things to do with her summer.

She finally spotted the shovel. It lay on the rock pile that covered the base of the big boulder. She'd never paid attention to the house-sized rock because the cabin was the real magnet for her attention. The top of the boulder was wider than the bottom, though it was hard to tell, because of the pile of rocks up against it. In the rocks, by her shovel, she noticed a piece of log sticking out. The log, only a few inches across, was cut flat at the end.

As Tyra picked up the shovel, an idea sprung to life. Warmth and energy flowed back into her muscles.

"What if they didn't dig a hole?" she asked quietly.

"What?" Grandpa Rudy growled.

"This pile of rocks doesn't look like it belongs here."

"The woods are full of rocks and boulders. The glaciers left big piles of them after the ice age."

"The ice age didn't put lumber in those piles. Not cut logs, anyway."

Grandpa Rudy grabbed a lantern and joined Tyra.

"You think they buried the safe under here?"

"What if they buried the whole car?" Tyra could imagine Uncle Danny behind the wheel, driving the big green car under the overhang of the boulder. "Maybe these rocks weren't usually here, and they normally parked the car under the shelf of this giant rock, kind of like a garage," Tyra continued.

She walked around the pile of rocks. There were larger rocks on the side, but none so big they couldn't have been placed there by a strong man. Grandpa Rudy raised his lantern. Through a gap in the stones, they could see the suggestion of a wall of rough-cut lumber.

"So the treasure was never in a hole at all?"

"Maybe not. Maybe they made this look like a big natural pile of rocks. But usually the front was open or had a cover of wood, like a garage door. On that day, they piled up stones in front to hide it. But no one ever came back. And no one ever found it, because the treasure hunters were digging holes in the ground instead of pulling down walls." Now that Tyra had her own story, she understood what kept Grandpa Rudy digging.

"What do you think?" she asked.

"I think I like your story a lot," he said. "Let's see if it's true."

He set down his lantern and started pulling rocks off the pile.

Tyra was sure it was the right story. But if there was no treasure here, maybe she'd become like Grandpa Rudy and never stop searching. She'd grow old and wrinkly, and spend every night out here digging or poking through rock piles, with slimy teeth and twigs and leaves stuck in her braids.

Together they pried and rolled away the stones from the top of the pile. It didn't take long to discover that there was only one layer of rocks. Underneath was a wall of wood.

"I think you might be right," Grandpa Rudy said, breathing hard. "That old stone wall that snakes along the road should continue all the way to this boulder, but see how it stops about thirty yards out? They must have covered the garage door with rocks from that wall."

They pushed away more and more rocks, faster and faster, their fingers scraped and numbed by the rough granite. Finally, they'd exposed an expanse of wood that was nearly three feet square. Grandpa Rudy walked across the clearing and retrieved his pick. As Tyra held a lantern, he swung the tool at the wall, and the wood gave way.

The dank air seeped out of the hole they'd made. Tyra extended the lantern up to the opening.

A giant green car, covered with dust and bits of rock, stared back at them.

Chapter Nineteen

Tyra and Grandpa Rudy pried and pulled away the layers of stones and wood until they opened a large enough space for them to crawl inside. The roof of the garage/cave was barely tall enough for the car, and Grandpa Rudy had to hunch over. Carefully constructed walls of logs and stones lined the back and side, leaving just enough room for a person to get out of the car.

The curvaceous Cadillac sat in the dim lantern light. On both sides, they could see where the mirrors had broken off. The rear door handle on the driver's side was missing. Grandpa Rudy walked forward and gently touched the car. Tyra wondered how it felt to make contact with something that had only been a fantasy, year after year. She stepped forward to the driver's side window and tried to rub away the dust and grit coating the glass. It was so dark, she couldn't make out the seats or steering wheel. "Do you think there's anything inside?" Tyra asked.

"If I didn't, would I have spent thirty years looking for it?"

Tyra hoped the safe would be inside, but she wasn't as certain as Grandpa Rudy. The fact that he'd searched for so long didn't make it any more likely that it would be there. Maybe they should put all the stones back and hide it again. What if just looking for a treasure is what makes it worth something? Opening the car could never be as good as what they'd imagined, could it? If they just left it there, they'd know they'd found it, but would never have to worry about all the stuff that might come afterward.

Nah. If there was treasure inside, Tyra wanted to see it.

Grandpa Rudy stared at the driver's door, his hand almost, but not quite, touching the handle. Not yet.

"Are you sure you want to open it?" Tyra asked.

"Are you afraid something scary might be in there?"

She hesitated. "What if there's nothing inside?"

He smiled. "I've dug a lot of holes and found disappointment at the bottom of each one. Don't worry, I can handle whatever we discover. You don't get to be as old as I am without growing a tough skin."

He put his hand on the latch and pulled. It didn't budge. He yanked again. And again.

Suddenly, the door flew open and a human skeleton in a moth-eaten business suit tumbled out onto the ground. Tyra screamed.

"Shhh!" Grandpa said, clasping a hand over her mouth. "Don't let the whole world know we're here."

Tyra squelched the rest of her screams, making high-pitched squeaks instead, as she stood petrified, pointing at the bones that had fallen out of the car. Grandpa Rudy picked up the dusty fedora that had rolled off the skull. He poked his finger through a hole in the side of the hat.

"Bullet hole," he said.

"Who . . . Who . . . Who is that?" Tyra stammered.

"I'm not sure. But I have a hunch." He gently pulled open the skeleton's suit jacket and felt the inside pocket. He pulled out a playing card—an ace of spades.

"Say hello to your great-great-uncle Danny."

Chapter Twenty

Tyra pushed the empty wheelbarrow over to Grandpa Rudy, who was carrying the skeleton out of the cave. She'd never seen an actual dead person before, though she and Adriana and Déjà had seen the bloodstain on the sidewalk after Jamal Brock was shot, not two blocks from her house. A shrine of stuffed animals, empty liquor bottles, and candles had been placed, with the words *RIP Mad Dog* scrawled on the pavement.

She thought back to all the ghost stories Walter had told at the lodge. What would he think of these bones? Did Uncle Danny's ghost lurk around here somewhere? Was he really murdered by Emerald Eddie? The white skull glowed in the lamplight.

Grandpa Rudy filled the wheelbarrow with the bones of his long-lost uncle. "Too bad I never got to meet him. Running with the wrong crowd isn't good for a long life, I guess. We can give him a proper burial later. Why don't you put him over by the cabin for now?"

Tyra didn't move. She wasn't about to go anywhere near that skeleton. Pushing a wheelbarrow full of old bones might give her nightmares for life. "Oh, no, I can't. Please don't make me. Please, please, *please.*"

For once, Grandpa Rudy seemed to understand. He pushed the wheelbarrow over by the old rumrunners' cabin and carefully placed the bones on the ground under a spruce tree, where they'd be protected. Tyra was glad that, even though he wanted his treasure, he showed a little care with the remains of Uncle Danny.

On his way back, Grandpa Rudy brought their biggest flashlight and another lantern. They climbed back through the hole and prepared to enter the car. Tyra followed close behind him. He hesitated.

"Now or never, right?" He took a deep breath and climbed inside. Tyra held out her lantern, trying not to breathe in the smell of old bones that hung like an invisible cloud.

"Any more skeletons?"

His voice was muffled in the buried car. "Don't worry—no more bodies. There's something way in the back, though. But it's under a blanket." He crawled over the front seat.

Tyra climbed inside, scrambled over the driver's seat, and joined her grandfather in the spacious rear section of the Cadillac. In the stillness, Tyra thought she could hear the sound of their thumping hearts.

This car was like nothing she'd ever seen before, with wood trim, white leather walls, and green velvet seats. It must have been the height of luxury in the 1920s. Now the coverings were tinged with mold and rot. On the broad expanse of carpeted floor between the front and back seats something rested under a gray wool blanket. Slowly, Grandpa Rudy pulled off the covering to reveal a cube of steel not quite a foot and a half on each side. Emerald Eddie's safe.

If they hadn't been buried under rocks and logs, their shouts of joy would have echoed all the way to Spirit Lake Lodge and woken the guests.

Grandpa Rudy ran his fingers across the top of the strongbox. Year after year of searching. Of doubting. All of it showed on his face.

On the door to the safe was a black combination lock and a shiny steel handle. Could Emerald Eddie have left it unlocked?

"Try the handle," Tyra said.

Grandpa Rudy took Tyra's suggestion, but the handle didn't move. They sat in the car for a while and stared at the safe.

"We have to get this out of here. Who knows how many other people are out looking," Grandpa Rudy said. Tyra felt guilty—if she and Cory hadn't shown the mirror to everyone at the lodge, maybe no one else would be searching.

"I'm not sure how we'll get it open," Grandpa Rudy continued, "but once we bring it back to the barn, I'll try every tool I have."

A sound came through the open front door of the car.

"Did you hear something?" Tyra whispered.

"Shhh." Grandpa Rudy crouched low and crawled into the front seat.

Another sound, like the rattle of old bones. Was something messing with Uncle Danny's skeleton? Or had it come to life?

"There's someone out there," Grandpa Rudy said in a low voice.

They peered through the dusty windshield, unable to see anything other than the glow of the morning sun. Was it the person who'd broken into the house? A person who wanted this safe and would stop at nothing to get it?

"What should we do?" Tyra asked.

"Stay low and very still. If they come to the opening, I'll rush them."

Tyra dug into her pocket and found her whistle. "I can blow this. It might scare them off. And I have this, too." She showed him her pocketknife. He took it and opened it.

"It's not much, but it'll do. Hush. Maybe they'll miss it."

This time, the sound of rocks on rocks. Someone had found the pile and the opening. A shadow flitted across the dusty windshield.

"Here I go," Grandpa Rudy whispered.

The shadow stopped in front of the opening. Someone was looking at the car, about to come in.

Grandpa Rudy jumped out of the car, pocketknife in hand, and leaped right at the figure in the opening to the garage, as Tyra blew hard on her whistle. *Tweet! Tweet! Tweet!*

"Don't kill me!" Tyra heard Cory's voice pleading.

She rushed from the car to see Grandpa Rudy standing over Cory, who had fallen to the ground, scared senseless. Grandpa Rudy's whole body shook. He let the pocketknife slip from his fingers and closed his eyes.

Tyra rushed to Cory. "Are you all right?"

"No! You guys almost scared me to death."

The feeling came back to Tyra's tingling fingers, and she could swallow again. Her lungs happily drew in air, like they'd been underwater for an hour.

"What are you doing here?" Grandpa Rudy demanded, his eyes burning with anger.

"I was looking for Tyra. I haven't seen her for days. I thought maybe she ran away and came to the cabin."

"How did you get here?"

"In my boat. It's anchored in Crescent Bay."

Grandpa Rudy looked like he was in pain. "I almost hurt you, Cory. If anything had happened to you, Lily would never have forgiven me. I never would've forgiven myself. I'm sorry."

"It's okay," Tyra said. "He's fine. We're all fine."

Grandpa Rudy nodded and frowned again. "Who else knows you're here?"

"Nobody. I told my grandmother I was going fishing."

Tyra stepped between them and helped Cory up. "It's okay," she said soothingly. "Cory can keep a secret." She believed it fully when she said it, but upon reflection, she wasn't sure. He could get so excited and didn't always think before speaking.

"Cross my heart and all that. I promise and swear and guarantee complete and total silence. My lips are sealed. Did you find Emerald Eddie's treasure? Is that his car? Where did those bones come from? Are they real?"

Grandpa Rudy rubbed his tired eyes and sighed. "Go ahead. Show him."

Tyra guided Cory around the car, shined a light on the safe, and told him all about Uncle Danny. Cory was so excited, he was twitching. "I can't believe any of this is real. Real buried treasure. A real bullet hole. A real skeleton. Now, *that's* an adventure!"

Cory crawled into the car with a flashlight to see the safe. When he crawled back out, Grandpa Rudy stood in front of him, close, intimidating, looking down at him with narrowed eyes. "If you breathe a word about this to anyone, even your grandmother, I will stick you in that car and wall it up again. Understand?"

Cory swallowed hard. "Yes, sir."

"Since you're here, we might as well put you to work. Let's get this opening cleared so we can push the wheelbarrow inside."

Together, the three of them moved all the rocks and logs away from the entrance to the hidden garage. They pushed the wheelbarrow alongside the car and opened the passenger door. Tyra hoped Uncle Danny's ghost would leave the car, now that the doors were open. At the very least, air could flow through and flush out the odor of bottled darkness.

The safe was heavy, but Grandpa Rudy was able to roll it end over end across the floor of the car. Each time the safe rolled, they could hear something inside, moving. To Tyra it sounded like gold clanking against emeralds.

Grandpa Rudy tied a rope around the safe and together the three of them heaved and pulled, huffing and puffing, to pull it into the bowl of the wheelbarrow. The wheelbarrow creaked under its heavy burden but didn't collapse as Grandpa Rudy wheeled the safe out into the daylight.

Then they sat on an old fallen log on the edge of the clearing and celebrated with three sodas, now warm from the summer heat, and a pile of sandwiches that Cory had brought in case he got hungry.

"What do you think is inside?" asked Cory, as he devoured a second turkey sandwich.

"Gold," said Tyra.

"Supposedly there's gold and cash inside. And some gems— he really did have a thing for emeralds." Grandpa Rudy crunched a carrot and stared at the safe.

"I've never seen an emerald," Cory said.

"Maybe that can be your share," Grandpa Rudy said.

"My share?"

"You're working hard. You've earned something."

Tyra wondered if she'd get something, too. Maybe her parents could have some. How would Grandpa Rudy use his share?

"The hard part is yet to come—we have to cart this all the way back to the cabin." Grandpa Rudy rose to his feet. "Come on," he said. "We don't want this out in the open."

Chapter Twenty-One

Grandpa Rudy crept out of the woods into the yard by the barn. "Keep out of sight," he whispered. "And don't make a sound until I give the all clear."

Tyra and Cory watched from the underbrush as Grandpa Rudy straightened himself out and tried to look carefree, innocently whistling and jauntily swinging his shovel. He checked inside the barn. Nothing. He started walking across the grass between the barn and the cabin, when Lily suddenly rose from one of the lawn chairs outside the back porch. She marched right up to Grandpa Rudy.

"Rudy Palmer! Where is your granddaughter?"

"Hello, Lily. Fine day, isn't it?"

"Don't you 'fine day' me! Cory mentioned the lies you told him about Tyra being sick with the frog flu. And now she's vanished. I know you two don't always see eye to eye, but she's just a girl. Do you have her locked up in there?"

"She's, uh. . . out playing in the woods. Probably with Cory."

"No. He went searching for her this morning. Told me he was going fishing, but I know better. Have you got her chained up out there digging holes?"

"Are you accusing me? Now, Lily. You know me."

"I thought I did. But you've got your eye somewhere else, and sometimes you don't think straight. Men can get that way, when something shiny catches their eye."

"She's out in the woods, Lily. I swear. She likes to explore. That's all. And she actually was sick, for a bit. I was just kidding Cory about the frog flu."

"You're a real joker," Lily said, her mouth a firm line. "You'd better produce Tyra and yourself at dinner tonight, or I'll call the state police and have them scour these woods and drag the lake until we find her. Do you understand me?"

"I do." He wiped the sweat from his brow. "We'll both be there. You don't need to worry. Not about anything."

"Don't disappoint me, Rudy. Not this time." Lily looked at him quizzically, as if she'd suddenly noticed something different about him. But then she shook her head and walked quickly back to her boat.

Grandpa Rudy watched Lily drive away until she was no more than a speck on the other side of the lake, almost back to town. "The coast is clear," he called.

Tyra and Cory pushed the wheelbarrow out of the woods and into the barn. It squeaked, and the wheel wobbled under the weight of the safe and from having been smacked on rocks. Whenever they'd had to drag it up a steep hill, they'd wrapped ropes around the safe and then around two trees at the top to help it along. The way home had been harder than they'd expected, but when Tyra's blazes started appearing on the trees, they knew they'd make it.

Grandpa Rudy flicked on the barn's overhead lights and slid the door shut. "This door stays shut and locked. From now on, we only use the side door, got it?"

The kids nodded.

"Why don't you go jump in the lake and get cleaned up. If people see you looking like walking mud piles, they're going to ask questions. Then take our boat to fetch Cory's, so he can hurry home before Lily thinks I've murdered him, too."

After all they'd been through, Tyra felt like the treasure was partly hers. She didn't want to miss the opening of the safe. "But I want to see what's inside."

"Don't worry, it'll take a while to get my tools ready. And since we're going to the lodge for dinner, I need to clean myself up, too."

"We are?" Tyra was shocked.

"If I don't personally deliver you there tonight, the woods will be crawling with snoops. Lily's a woman who follows through on her promises. It's one of her many qualities that are both wonderful and annoying. I suppose I can stomach being social for an hour or two, if it keeps prying eyes away."

Tyra and Cory ran down to the shore and jumped into the lake in their shorts and T-shirts. The icy water numbed their aching muscles and soaked out some of the tiredness from digging and hauling. They scrubbed off all the grit and grime from the day, and then floated on their backs, staring at the puffy clouds. Tyra thought of her parents, strolling beneath the Eiffel Tower in Paris. What would they say if they knew she'd helped find Emerald Eddie's treasure?

#

When she got back to the house after dropping Cory at his boat, Tyra changed into her best clean shirt and shorts and went out to the barn. She could hear drilling and muttering inside, but the side door was locked. She knocked loudly.

"Who is it?"

"It's me."

"Me who?"

"Tyra, your granddaughter."

She could hear him on the other side of the door. "What's the password?"

Password? "There is no password."

The door opened, and she followed Grandpa Rudy to the center of the barn, where the safe lay on the floor with bright shop lights surrounding it.

"You didn't open it yet, did you?"

"Not for lack of trying. Sorry, I couldn't wait. It was just sitting there, taunting me."

Drills and hammers and saws lay scattered across the concrete floor. Grandpa Rudy wore a shirt with a collar and khaki pants and clean boots. His hair was combed, and he'd trimmed his beard. He appeared to be a pleasant old grandfather, not a scary mountain man.

"You look nice," Tyra said.

"Thought I'd better make myself presentable if I have to subject myself to the whole social scene. Try to blend in and not seem so much like a crazy treasure hunter."

Tyra figured that Grandpa Rudy showing up all normal looking would be more suspicious than anything else he could possibly do, but she didn't want to say anything. She wouldn't mind people seeing that he could look like a regular person every once in a while.

"Have you tried any of these yet?" she asked, pointing at the tools.

"I tried the drill, but even my hardened steel bits keep breaking. See?"

He put on his safety glasses and pressed the drill against the steel door. It spun and spun without making a scratch. With a little more pressure, the bit snapped.

"I tried guessing the combination, but it's hopeless. It may be old, but it's a solid piece of work."

Tyra turned the dial on the safe. She pressed her ear against it as she turned the black knob back and forth, like she'd seen in her dad's old movies, but she couldn't tell if the clicking and spinning inside meant anything. She jiggled the handle, but it didn't budge. All that effort and now it wouldn't open. How would they ever find a way?

"We have our work cut out for us tonight," Grandpa Rudy said. "But first we need to keep those snoops out of our business."

#

Subject: Should we call the police?

Hi Tyra,

You disappeared again! Where are you?! Should we call the police? Are you really treasure hunting? Did you find it? Or did something happen?

Nothing is happening here. Except Danté told Déjà that he likes her, but Déjà said she won't go out with him. I think he's cute, but she thinks he smells funny.

Write to us soon, or we'll have to call in the detectives to find you.

Love, Adriana

Subject: You'll never guess!!!

Hi Adriana and Déjà!
Can't write for long, my grandfather is waiting. I'm okay. More tired than you can imagine. Can't tell you what happened, except that it's a BIG SECRET. DON'T BREATHE A WORD, or we could be in great danger.

Bye. Love, T

#

When Tyra and Grandpa Rudy walked into the dining room, Lily almost dropped her tray of fried chicken at the sight of them. "Will wonders never cease? Rudy Palmer, in the flesh. My goodness, don't you look very ... handsome." Grandpa Rudy flushed bright red and rubbed his beard nervously as he followed Tyra to their seats. Lily watched the two of them closely, unable to take her eyes off the new Rudy Palmer.

Once Cory had finished helping carry out the dinner, he sat next to Tyra. "Did you get in trouble?" Tyra asked.

"Not much. A couple extra chores, that's it. Did you do it? The thing? Did it happen?" Cory was whispering, but Grandpa Rudy shot him a severe look of warning, and Cory shut himself up with a dinner roll. It would take every ounce of self-control for Cory to keep this secret.

Tyra focused on her salad but talked quietly out of the corner of her mouth. "Nothing yet. Maybe tonight."

"Can I sleep over?"

Grandpa Rudy was busy laughing with Walter and Ted over yet another fish story. Tyra turned to her grandfather and whispered in his ear, "Can Cory spend the night?" He started to shake his head no, but she quickly added, "It's the best way to keep him quiet." Grandpa Rudy gave Tyra a little nod.

The three treasure hunters ate as if they'd been without food for a week. Digging all night and hauling a heavy safe through the woods had built a powerful appetite.

Tyra's head bobbed a little as she struggled to stay awake. The food and the warm buzz of the dining room were lulling her to sleep.

"I'm glad to know you all like my fried chicken so much," Lily said with a laugh. "But that poor girl can barely keep her eyes open. What sort of hard labor have you got her doing?"

"It's okay," Tyra said. "I've just been helping out. Doing chores. But I'm about done, right, Grandpa?" She almost dozed off in the middle of her sentence.

Grandpa Rudy clapped her warmly on the shoulder. "That's right. Never expected her to be such a hard worker. Started out as a city girl, but now she's A-OK."

"I think I know what sort of work you've been having her do," Walter boomed.

"Do you?"

"Probably the same thing as Becky and Tim."

All eyes turned to the honeymooners, who both flushed. Becky glanced down shyly.

"I don't know many lovebirds who go on picnics with shovels," Walter continued. "Show us those hands, Becky. Go on now."

Becky reluctantly revealed her red, blistered palms. Tim pulled them back under the table. "Just having a little fun," Tim said.

"We didn't find anything except rocks," Becky said, with a touch of bitterness.

"Perhaps digging for buried treasure is not what she had in mind for her honeymoon," teased Meredith.

"Guess you're not the only one out there digging, Rudy," said Walter, his eyes bright under his bushy brows.

"I don't know what you're talking about," said Rudy.

The other guests at the table laughed.

Lily was not amused. "Oh, Rudy, Tyra's on her summer vacation. Honey, you need to come stay with us for a few days. Seriously, Rudy. She could come stay for a bit. You're working her too hard. Especially if you've got her involved in all that foolishness."

"I need a vacation, too, Grandma," Cory said.

Lily swatted him playfully with a wooden serving spoon, as she passed the green beans over to Meredith. "You get a vacation when I get a vacation. What do you say, Tyra? We had a family leave a few days early, so there's an extra cabin."

Tyra loved the idea of a cozy cabin all her own, but not yet. "I would really like that. But not tonight. I have to finish a project with Grandpa."

Lily raised her eyebrows in surprise.

"Grandma, can I go spend the night at Mr. Palmer's place?" Cory asked.

"I don't imagine he'd—"

"That'd be great," Rudy said. "There's a cot on the porch he can use. And this way Tyra won't talk my ear off until past my bedtime. They wanted to get in some early-morning fishing, isn't that right?"

The kids nodded eagerly, but Lily looked skeptical.

"Don't worry. I'll make sure they get a decent breakfast. Nothing like you'd make, of course. The chicken is out of this world. And these biscuits. Heaven."

Tyra thought he was laying it on a little thick, but Lily agreed that Cory could go.

"Are you heading out to the secret fishing spot?" Ted asked. "Down by Loon Point?"

"You know about that?" Cory said.

"Some say you're the best fisherman on the lake, Cory. We all notice where you fish."

"Sure we do," Walter chimed in. "You have a reputation."

Tyra looked at Ted and Walter suspiciously. It seemed like everyone in Spirit Lake was watching everyone else. And there was Meredith, leaning toward them, listening too intently. Tyra was exhausted, but she studied each of the lodge guests closely. Was Ted laughing a little too loudly? And why was Walter suddenly acting like he was old pals with Grandpa Rudy?

Cory smiled modestly. "Aw, well, I try."

Walter added another clean drumstick to the growing pile on his plate. "Did you catch much while you were out today? Your grandma said you were out fishing most of the day."

"Oh, I, uh, didn't have much luck today. I mean, I caught a bunch, but they were all too small. Still trying to catch a fallfish."

Tyra watched Cory, hoping she wouldn't have to jump in to keep him from saying too much. She couldn't blame him for wanting to say something. She wanted to scream, "We found it! We found it!" But she kept it bottled inside.

The arrival of strawberry shortcake saved the day—everyone focused on dessert. Tyra kicked Cory under the table to warn him to be more careful.

#

Lily packed Cory a little duffel bag with clean underwear, dry swim trunks, and a toothbrush. "Don't get Tyra into any more trouble," she warned Cory as he jumped into the boat. "And don't annoy Mr. Palmer. If that's possible."

"Don't worry, Lily," Grandpa Rudy said, laughing. "I won't be too tough on the boy."

Lily frowned. "I don't know what's come over you, Rudy. Are you feeling all right?" She looked closely into Grandpa Rudy's eyes, and, for once, he didn't look away.

"I can honestly say I've never felt better."

"I owe you an apology. This afternoon, I was out of line. You surprised me tonight. I'm glad."

"I might have one or two more surprises for you. Try to be patient with me a little longer. I know I've made a lot of mistakes. But maybe it's not too late."

This time it was Lily's turn to stammer and blink. "I think . . . I think . . ."

"Good night, Lily. You're a fine woman, and it would take a lot for a man to be worthy of you." He placed both hands on her shoulders, kissed her on the cheek, and jumped down into the boat. "Turn on that lantern, kids. We'd better get you home to bed."

He steered them off into the night with a wave at Lily, who stood on the dock, watching them. She faded into the shadows, a look of puzzlement and longing on her face.

Chapter Twenty-Two

They tried every single one of Grandpa Rudy's tools. He pulled out hacksaws, a circular saw, a reciprocating saw. He showed them how to light a propane blowtorch, and they tried to burn a hole through the steel. The sledgehammer just bounced off. Tyra slammed a sharp-ended mattock against the steely face, with no effect. Cory pounded a chisel with a hammer against the crack of the safe's door. Nothing worked.

Grandpa Rudy found some steel wedges that he used for splitting wood and ground them to a fine edge on his grinder in a shower of sparks. Cory and Tyra held the wedges as Grandpa Rudy tapped at them with the sledgehammer, but no matter how sharp the end, they penetrated only a few millimeters into the safe.

"What if we use dynamite?" Cory suggested. "Isn't that what they do in the movies?"

"But we'd blow up whatever's inside," Tyra said.

"Or blow ourselves to smithereens. Tempting, but I don't think so," Grandpa Rudy said.

They stared and stared at the safe, and it just sat there, unyielding. Grandpa Rudy paced around the barn, muttering, "Stupid, stupid, stupid. Why didn't I buy a cutting torch?"

Cory's eyes drooped after the long day of adventure, and Tyra wasn't much more awake.

"What if we do judo on it?" she suggested groggily.

"Karate-chop it open?" Cory said. He did a fake karate chop on the safe. "*Hi-ya!*"

"No," said Tyra. "What if we use the safe to open itself? It's strong and heavy, which is why we can't open it. But what if we use the fact that it's strong and heavy to open it?"

Grandpa Rudy stopped pacing and started listening.

Tyra continued, "We could pick it up and drop it. Either onto the floor or onto something pointy, like a sharp piece of steel or a rock. We could hook it up to those beams." She pointed up at the exposed rafters of the barn.

"That's a fantastic idea," Grandpa Rudy said. "Let's give it a try."

He tied strong knots around the safe, while the kids grabbed the ladder. Tyra scrambled up and passed the end of the rope over a pulley that hung from the highest beam. She looked down for a second and realized how high up she was. If she fell now, she'd definitely crack open. Maybe the safe would, too.

They heaved and pulled and lifted the safe into the air. It swung back and forth as it inched higher and higher until it almost touched the roof of the barn.

Tyra and Cory gave the countdown. "Five, four, three, two, one. Go!"

They released the rope and ducked behind the snowplow blade. The safe crashed down with a bang louder than thunder. It bounced off the floor and knocked into Grandpa Rudy's workbench, like a bowling ball smashing into bowling pins.

"Woo-hoo!" Tyra and Cory shouted.

They rushed to see if they'd revealed Emerald Eddie's treasure.

The safe was still locked tight. One corner was slightly scratched and dented. That was it.

"No way," Cory protested.

Grandpa Rudy's face was grim. "I can have a cutting torch in a day or two."

Cory's shoulders slumped. "Two days?"

"Until then, I guess we'll keep trying with what we've got," Grandpa Rudy said.

Tyra wasn't sure they'd ever find the right way. Maybe it would stay locked forever. They would look at it every day and wonder: what's inside?

Grandpa Rudy slid the safe back to the middle of the barn, where he resumed hammering at the door with whatever he could find. He pounded at the strongbox with every ounce of frustration in his body.

Chapter Twenty-Three

"Keep your hands where I can see them."

Tyra blinked and rubbed her eyes. The old inflatable raft in the corner of the barn, where she'd lain down to sleep, crinkled and clicked as she shifted to see what was happening. Nearby, on another old raft, Cory snorted in his sleep.

Grandpa Rudy stood absolutely still by the safe, holding his hands in the air. Ted leaned through the side door, in the shadows. He inched forward, and light glinted off the barrel of a shiny pistol in his hand.

"Ted, what are you doing?" Grandpa Rudy spoke calmly, though Tyra could tell he was angry and a little afraid.

"I see you over there, Tyra. You and Cory stay put." Ted spoke to Tyra, but he kept his eyes on Grandpa Rudy. Cory started to stretch awake, and as soon as his eyes were open, Tyra put her finger to her lips to shush him.

"How did you know?" Grandpa Rudy asked.

Ted came all the way inside and closed the door. "I've been watching you for years, every summer. When Tyra found the mirror, I figured you were close. Everyone else got all worked up, stupid Walter and Meredith, and even those silly honeymooners. Digging all over the place. But they had no idea what they were doing. I wasn't worried about them. If anyone was going to find Emerald Eddie's stash, it would be you. I looked at your maps and through your files, but you were too careful to leave any clues.

"Then you disappeared for days. I knew something was up. This morning, I saw Cory's boat in Crescent Bay. I thought he'd gone to search for more antique bottles and hoped he'd lead me to the site. By the time I got there, you'd already left. The Cadillac was empty. I knew you must have the treasure here."

Grandpa Rudy didn't look like he planned to move away from the safe. "I've been searching for this for half my life."

"It doesn't belong to you." Even though his face was red and sweaty, Ted's green eyes were cold. "Emerald Eddie McCoy was my grandfather."

"Ted McCoy," whispered Cory. "That's his name."

"This safe is my inheritance. I heard all about it from my relatives. At every family gathering, someone would start talking about Emerald Eddie and his famous treasure, but none of those bums ever did a thing to find it. It was up to me. When I was finally old enough to start looking, you were already here, already searching. But I thought, hey, if Rudy wants to find it, let him. I'll make sure I'm there when he does. And you did. Thanks."

Grandpa Rudy put a hand on the safe and patted it gently. "We can't get it open."

"That's okay. It'd be simpler to just take the contents, but if I have to bring the whole thing, I can manage. I have old family friends back in New York with the skills for a project like this. It won't be the first safe they've opened. And they know how to keep quiet. Just like you will.

"If you tell anyone you found this, no one will believe you. And if you do say anything, you'd better hope I don't find you." Ted's evil tone clashed with his playful fishing vest and hat full of lures. Tyra could tell he was deadly serious.

Grandpa Rudy stepped away from the safe, toward the kids. "Go ahead. Take it." Tyra couldn't believe he would let Ted steal the safe. Shouldn't he leap into action like in the movies and grab a shovel and knock Ted out or something?

"Oh, I will. And since you're so good at lugging it around, you're going to put it on my boat. The kids will help."

"Don't bring them into this. You and me, we can get the safe wherever it needs to go. Just let them be." Grandpa Rudy inched over, so he now stood directly between Ted and the kids.

"They'll blab, first chance they get. If you don't do exactly as I say, there will be two fewer grandkids running around Spirit Lake."

Tyra and Cory lay absolutely still on their rafts. Ted walked to the center of the barn and touched the safe, as if to reassure himself it was real. He pushed at it, to see how heavy it was. It budged a little.

"It's smaller than I expected. But big enough to have a fortune inside. Come on, let's get this out to the dock."

A loud knock came from the side door. They all froze. Tyra hoped it was the police coming to their rescue.

Ted kept his gun pointed at Grandpa Rudy. "Who's that?" he hissed.

"I don't know. I wasn't expecting a flood of visitors at five in the morning."

Lily's voice came through the thick door. "Rudy Palmer, if you're in there, open up right this second!"

"Great. Just great," Ted muttered.

Tyra's heart sank—no rescue, and now Lily might get caught up in this whole mess.

"Rudy!"

Ted waved at Grandpa Rudy with the gun. "Open the door and get her in here. Don't you kids move a muscle."

They all did as they were told. Tyra wanted to shout for Lily to run away, but she didn't dare. Not as long as Ted was pointing a gun at her grandfather.

Lily stood in the open doorway, her hair tousled, though she was already wearing her jeans and work shirt. "Oh, Rudy. What's going on? I haven't been able to sleep a wink. You have suddenly transformed, like the years of worry and obsession have fallen away, and I don't understand what's happened. We need to talk about you and me. I'd lost hope, but now you've got me confused."

"Lily, now is not—"

"Whatever there is between us, it's time to finally take action. There. I said it. I'm here. You're here."

"Lily, listen . . ."

"And why is Ted's boat at your dock, but there's no sign of him or the kids?"

She finally looked past Grandpa Rudy and saw Ted with his gun.

Her eyes widened. "What's happening?"

"Get inside and be quiet," Ted said. "Now we'll have an extra pair of hands to help get that safe onto the boat. Come on, before it gets light out."

Lily stepped into the barn, scared, and Grandpa Rudy closed the door behind her. "Ted McCoy, what are you doing? Are you out of your mind?"

"I'm taking what's mine, and no one is going to stop me." With the angry sneer on his face, Ted wasn't a mild-mannered lodge guest anymore.

Lily noticed the safe lying on the floor in the center of the barn. Her eyes found Grandpa Rudy's. "Is that what I think it is?"

"I found it, Lily," Grandpa Rudy said. "After all these years. Actually, Tyra's the one who figured it out."

"Where are the children?" She spied Cory and Tyra in the corner. "Are you two okay?"

"I think so." Cory's voice sounded small and frightened. Tyra couldn't even bring herself to speak. When she opened her mouth, no sound came out.

"Ted. This is unacceptable. You cannot hold children at gunpoint. Let them go right this second." Lily's tough tone faded quickly. "Please?"

"Not until you put this safe on my boat," Ted said firmly. "Let's go!"

The kids pushed a sturdy two-wheeled garden cart over to the safe, and Grandpa Rudy tipped it down so they could maneuver the strongbox onto it.

Lily came over to join them, and Cory whispered to her, "He's Emerald Eddie's grandson."

"I had no idea," she said in a low voice. "He always seemed so nice. Shows how hard it is to tell what's really inside someone. Rudy, we can't trust him."

Grandpa Rudy whispered without even moving his lips. "He wouldn't be the first one in his family to kill to keep this treasure a secret. I've got to get that gun away from him."

Tyra thought about the hole in Uncle Danny's fedora and shivered.

"Stop chatting and get moving," Ted called from the open barn doors.

They tipped the cart back up onto its wheels, and it gave a loud metal creak. The safe still had ropes wrapped around it from when they'd dropped it.

"Bring those two wide boards, too." The sky was already beginning to lighten in the east. "Hurry. It'll be dawn soon."

#

Their parade wound its way to the dock, followed closely by Ted, who never let his gun waver. None of them dared make a move to escape. In the movies, it always looked so easy, but Tyra didn't see how they could do it. If she tried to get away, he might catch her or hurt Grandpa Rudy or Lily or Cory. Even Cory wasn't fast enough to outrun a bullet.

If only she'd never snuck away from her chores, taken Cory to the digging site, and run and found that mirror. Then none of this would be happening. If only, if only, if only. But she couldn't take any of it back.

Out on the dock, Ted had them place the boards so that they made a ramp down to the center of his boat. "I've already got my truck and boat trailer at the launch in town, ready to go," he said. "Now get it on there. Carefully. If it drops in the lake, I'll make you jump in and haul it out."

They tipped the cart down onto its front lip and pushed the safe onto the boards. Together, Grandpa Rudy, Cory, and Tyra slid the safe down into the bottom of the boat. Lily watched helplessly, her eyes flicking back and forth between the gun and the children. Now Emerald Eddie's treasure lay safely on board, with the ropes still tied to it, spread all around like the tentacles of a giant octopus. Ted looked at his four hostages as if trying to decide what to do with them.

"Go ahead," Grandpa Rudy said. "Take it and go. You won't hear from us again. It'll be like we never found it."

Tyra wondered how hard it would be to keep such a secret for the rest of her life. It was one thing to never admit that you were the one who spilled juice on the couch or not tell anyone that Adriana broke the teacher's iPhone. But this would be a big thing to bury in her mind. Wouldn't she need to tell her father that Grandpa Rudy wasn't entirely crazy?

"We won't say a word," said Lily.

"Even though you're the nicest innkeeper in the world, you've got a big mouth. So does your grandson. Rudy's been obsessed with this for decades, so he can't be trusted. He's traded friendships, relationships, blood and sweat to find this treasure. You think he can just let it go? As for our little black inner-city refugee, well, who knows what she's capable of?" said Ted.

"Watch what you say," Grandpa Rudy warned.

"Or what?" Ted pointed the gun at Grandpa Rudy's chest. "I thought you didn't approve. It didn't make any sense to you. 'Why would Dave and Amanda adopt a black girl?' Isn't that what you used to say down at the store?"

Tyra's fingers and toes went numb, and her stomach shrank into a little pit.

"I changed my mind. She's every bit my grandchild, just as much as Cory is Lily's. I'd trust her with my life. She means the world to me."

Inside, Tyra's emotions were on a giant roller coaster. Cold was now hot.

"Isn't that sweet? I don't care. Take this and cover their mouths. Sound carries over the water too easily." Ted tossed a roll of duct tape to Grandpa Rudy.

"I won't let you hurt them."

"I'm not going to hurt anyone. Not if you follow directions. I'm going to leave you on Piper's Island. You'll say you were having a picnic and your boat came unmoored. It will be found drifting somewhere across the lake. I'm sure someone will pick you up in a few hours. Do it."

Reluctantly, Grandpa Rudy covered the mouths of Lily, Cory, and Tyra. As he taped Tyra's mouth, he whispered, "When I give the signal, make as much noise as you can, all right?" She nodded.

Ted made Grandpa Rudy tie a long rope from the back of Ted's boat to the front of Lily's, so he could tow them. Then Lily, Tyra, and Cory climbed into Lily's boat. As Grandpa Rudy started to join them, Ted barked, "Not you, old man. You're coming with me. I don't want you trying anything. And you three—if you do anything funny, Grandpa Rudy becomes fish food."

Ted made Grandpa Rudy perch in the open center of the boat, near the safe, so Ted could sit at the back and steer. "Don't want you crashing us into a rock or anything."

The motor gave off a low *grrr* as it strained to carry the two men and the safe, and also tow Lily's boat. Ted steered them slowly away from the dock over the deep water toward Piper's Island.

Lily huddled on the back seat of her boat, her arm clasped tightly around Cory's shoulder. But the seat was too narrow for three, so Tyra sat alone on the center bench. Ted never pointed the gun away from Grandpa Rudy.

When they were halfway across the open water, the motor conked out. Ted cursed angrily. "What's happening?" He looked up at Grandpa Rudy, who barely suppressed a smile. "What did you do?"

Grandpa Rudy shrugged innocently. "I'm over here."

"It's not funny. If I can't get this started, I'll make you row us there." Ted turned to examine the motor, while keeping his gun trained on Grandpa Rudy. As soon as Ted's head was turned, Grandpa Rudy nodded at Tyra.

Tyra pounded her feet against the bottom of the boat and smacked the seat with her hands. The blows on the aluminum bench boomed across the lake like small thunder. Lily and Cory stared at Tyra in horror, but Tyra banged as hard as she could.

Angrier than ever, Ted looked up from the motor and swung his gun at Tyra. "Stop that, or I'll shoot all three of you."

Tyra stopped.

"Put that gun down. Now," Grandpa Rudy called.

Ted's boat suddenly tipped to one side. While Tyra had Ted distracted, Grandpa Rudy had grabbed the safe with both hands and tipped it up against the side of the boat. Now the veins and sinews of his arms stood out clearly from the strain of holding the heavy weight up against the gunwale. The strongbox balanced precariously on the thin strip of metal. "If you don't put that gun down, I'll push it over."

Now it was Ted's turn to be frozen with fear. "You wouldn't."

"It's a deep lake. The only one to ever see this treasure will be the ghost of your grandfather."

"You're bluffing."

"I won't allow you to hurt my people. Hurry, I can't hold this much longer. Put down the gun."

Water sloshed around the bottom of the boat at the men's feet. Tyra ripped the duct tape off her face, ready to scream. "On the count of three, it goes," Grandpa Rudy warned. "One. Two. Three."

Four pairs of stunned eyes watched Grandpa Rudy heave Emerald Eddie's safe up and out of the boat. As it splashed into the water, the ropes whipped over the edge behind it. The gun clattered in the bottom of the boat as Ted leaped across the bench and grabbed a loop in one of the ropes in a desperate attempt to save his grandfather's treasure. It pulled him over the side and into the water before he realized he'd better let go, but the line had tightened around his wrist. As the strong box plunged into the depths, it dragged Ted with it, down to the bottom of the lake.

They all stared at the smooth surface of the water as the sound of the splash dissipated into the early-morning silence. The world had suddenly stopped.

"Tyra, throw me your pocketknife," Grandpa Rudy commanded.

She pulled the knife out of her pocket and tossed it to him. Grandpa Rudy opened the blade and dove after Ted and the safe. Lily and Cory stripped the tape from their mouths.

After a long time, Grandpa Rudy burst up to the surface of the lake, the knife still in his hand, sputtering and gasping for breath. He swam over to Lily's boat, and they pulled him on board.

Tyra stared at the spot where the safe and Ted had entered the water. A few bubbles rose to the surface, and then all was still. The lake was an impervious mirror to the sky, hiding whatever lurked below.

"It's too deep. I couldn't save him," Grandpa Rudy said in a low voice. "It's just too deep."

Chapter Twenty-Four

After a while, Cory started the motor and drove them back to Grandpa Rudy's dock, with Ted's boat in tow behind them. No one knew what to say, not even Lily.

At the dock, Grandpa Rudy and Tyra got off and tied Ted's empty boat to the cleats. Cory blinked half-lidded eyes, as if he still wasn't fully awake, maybe hoping this had all been a horrible nightmare. Lily looked up at Grandpa Rudy. "I'll call the police," she said.

"I'm sorry, Lily. About a lot of things."

"Rudy. You are quite a man. Don't make any more apologies to me."

"There are a lot of things I'm ready to change now. You'll see."

The sun skimmed the trees and lit the surface of the water, casting a golden glow onto all of them. Cory waved an exhausted wave at Tyra as he drove his grandmother home.

Grandpa Rudy wrapped a strong arm around Tyra's shoulders as a fog of silence settled around them. The glassy lake reflected the empty sky, reflected the whole world.

"I'm never going in that water again," she said.

"I'd understand that."

"Will he be a ghost, like Emerald Eddie? I don't want to be haunted." Already, Tyra could imagine a string of sleepless nights, wondering when Ted McCoy might knock on her window.

"If he'd want to haunt anyone, it would be me," Grandpa Rudy said, still looking out at the lake, his face hard. "But he made his choice, Tyra. We all made our choices. As far as I'm concerned, all the ghosts in my life need to stay sunk with that safe."

"Did you sabotage his engine?"

"I know a few things about boats. And I knew I needed to wreck his plans, keep him off balance."

"How did you know he'd drop the gun?"

"He was the only person in the world who wanted that treasure more than I did. I knew how he felt and what he'd do to keep it."

"I'm sorry you'll never know what was inside."

He looked down at her, his gaze softening. "Maybe I'll always wonder. But searching for that box carried a heavy price, in ways that hurt a lot of people. I may not have that treasure, but I found something that kept me from ending up at the bottom of the lake. I guess Ted didn't have anyone like you to show him what really matters."

Tyra gripped his hand in hers. It was rough and strong. And warm. She'd been so certain this summer would turn into a complete and total disaster. She never expected that, after so much digging, she would finally find a grandfather.

Acknowledgements

This is a project that's been in the works for a long time. Joanna Stempfel-Volpe gave me comments early on that provided some important confidence. Molly Tinsley was very helpful as I brought this book back to life after a long time where I thought it would never see the light of day.

My fiction group was a huge help, reading multiple drafts and providing insightful comments. I am eternally grateful to Erin Cashman, Eileen Donovan-Krantz, Clare Dunsford, Diana Renn, Ted Rooney, Greg Lewis, Deb Vlock, and Julie Wu for their help and their friendship.

I'm thankful to my dear friend Jessica Tuccelli for many long conversations about books and family and writing, and a push to make this book better. David Valdes Greenwood gave me encouragement just when I needed it.

Diane Sepanski came in at the end with important editorial input, and Jin Suk crafted a cover that I adore.

As always, none of my writing would be possible without my wife, Tracy, who is a constant source of love and support and makes it all worthwhile.

About the Author

Patrick Gabridge is a novelist, playwright, and screenwriter. This is his first book for younger readers. His novels for adults are *Tornado Siren*, *Moving [a life in boxes]*, and *Steering to Freedom*. He's written many stage plays, including *Lost in Lexicon*, *Drift*, *Blinders*, and *Blood on the Snow*. His short plays are published by Playscripts, Brooklyn Publishers, Heuer, Smith & Kraus, and YouthPlays, and have been used by thousands of students around the world in production and competition.

Patrick grew up in Upstate New York, in a place not too different from Spirit Lake, where he spent a lot of time fishing (including for northern pike) with his friends. Now he's a father and lives with his family near Boston. He has a passion for history, and in his spare time, he likes to farm and fix up old houses.

You can read more about Patrick's work at www.gabridge.com.

Made in the USA
Coppell, TX
26 August 2021